Skill Sharpeners 3

for ESL Students

Judy DeFilippo
Charles Skidmore
Michael Walker

ADDISON-WESLEY PUBLISHING COMPANY
Reading, Massachusetts • Menlo Park, California • Don Mills, Ontario
Amsterdam • London • Manila • Singapore • Sydney • Tokyo

Judy DeFilippo is Coordinator of ESL in the Intensive English program at Northeastern University.

Charles Skidmore is an ESL teacher at the secondary level in the Boston, Massachusetts, schools.

Michael Walker is the author of *New Horizons in English, Yes!, Step Ahead,* and other ESL series and texts.

Illustrations by Kathleen Todd: pp. 9, 14, 16, 20, 24, 25, 27, 32, 43, 51, 62, 68, 83, 85, 89, 93, 111, 112, 113

Other illustrations by Dave Blanchette and Larry Matteson

Cover design by Marshall Henrichs and Richard Hannus

Composition by Bookwrights, Inc.

Copyright © 1984 by Addison-Wesley Publishing Company, Inc. Philippines copyright 1984. All rights reserved. No part of this publication may be reproduced, stored in a retrieval system, or transmitted in any form or by any means, electronic, mechanical, photocopying, recording, or otherwise, without the prior written permission of the publisher. Printed in the United States of America.

DEFGHIJ-WC-898765
ISBN: 0-201-15633-4

Introduction

The *Skill Sharpeners* series has been especially designed for Junior High and Senior High School students who are coping with a new language and a new culture. By introducing basic skills tied to classroom subjects, in a simple, easy-to-understand ESL grammatical framework, the series helps to bridge the gap between ESL and regular academic subjects. By developing and reinforcing school and life survival skills, it helps build student confidence and success. Although designed specifically to accompany the Second Edition of *New Horizons in English*, the *Skill Sharpeners* can be used to supplement and complement any basic ESL series. They may also be used to reteach and reinforce specific skills with which students are having difficulty; to review and practice grammatical structures; and to reinforce, expand, and enrich students' vocabularies.

The grammatical structures in the *Skill Sharpeners* reflect the systematic, small-step progression that is a key feature of the *New Horizons* textbooks. The vocabulary and skill presentation, however, expand the text material with concepts and situations that have an immediate impact on students' daily lives and with themes and subject matter directly related to curriculum areas. Reading and study skills are stressed in many pages, and writing skills are carefully developed, starting with single words and sentences and building gradually to paragraphs and stories in a structured controlled-composition sequence.

You will find that some pages deviate from the structural presentation in the *New Horizons* texts in order accurately to present their important content. You should not expect most students to be able actively to use the structures on these pages in speaking or writing, but students should, however, be able to read and respond to the content. Do not be concerned about structural errors during discussion of the material. It is important that students become *actively involved* and *communicating*, however imperfectly, from the very beginning.

Using the *Skill Sharpeners*

Because each page or pair of pages of the *Skill Sharpeners* books is independent and self contained, the series lends itself to great flexibility in use. Teachers may pick and choose pages that fit the needs of particular students, or they may use the pages in sequential order. Most pages are self explanatory, and all are easy to use, either in class or as homework assignments. Detailed annotations on each page identify the skill or skills being developed and suggest ways to prepare for, introduce, and present the exercise(s) on the page. In most cases, oral practice of the material is suggested before the student is asked to complete the page in writing. Teacher demonstration and student involvement and participation help build a foundation for completing the page successfully and learning the skill.

The *Skill Sharpeners* are divided into thematic units. In Books 1 and 2, these correspond to the units of the *New Horizons* texts. In addition, each of the *Skill Sharpeners* books opens with a review/transition/orientation unit. In *Skill Sharpeners 1*, this unit provides introductory exercises to familiarize students with basic classroom language, school deportment, the names of various school areas and school personnel, number names, time and calendar names, and words for feelings and common requests. In later books of the series, the introductory unit serves both to review some of the material taught in earlier books and to provide orientation to the series for students coming to it for the first time.

At the end of each of the *Skill Sharpeners* books is a review of vocabulary and an end-of-book test of grammatical and reading skills. The test, largely in multiple-choice format, not only assesses learning of the skills but also serves as practice for other multiple-choice tests. The use of multiple-choice questions is developed in a number of the exercises in the first *Skill Sharpeners* book and is reinforced in the later books in the series.

The complete Table of Contents in each book identifies the skills developed on each page. A Skills Index at the end of the book lists skills alphabetically by topic and indicates the pages on which they are developed.

Skill Sharpeners invite expansion! We encourage you to use them as a springboard and to add activities and exercises that build on those in the books to fill the needs of your own particular students. Used this way, the *Skill Sharpeners* can significantly help to build the confidence and skills that students need to be successful members of their new community and successful achievers in their subject-area classrooms.

Contents

Starting Out

A Busy Morning *(Reviewing present tense, third person singular)* — 9

Small Talk *(Reviewing verb tenses, understanding cause and effect, building vocabulary, charting information)* — 10

The New Apartment *(Building vocabulary, identifying main idea, writing a descriptive paragraph)* — 11

Two Hundred Years of American History *(Interpreting a time line, identifying main idea, sequencing)* — 12

Affirmative and Negative *(Forming negative statements, asking questions)* — 13

UNIT 1   Discovering Facts and Feelings

Likes and Dislikes *(Using like(s), doesn't/don't like + gerund)* — 14

Yes or No? *(Asking/answering questions: Can . . .? Do/Does/Did . . .? Is/Are/Was/Were . . .?)* — 15

Choose the Best Word *(Choosing the correct verb tense and form: simple present and past, present and past progressive)* — 16

Alternative Word Meanings *(Choosing the correct definition, building vocabulary)* — 17

More Than a Name *(Identifying main idea and details, building vocabulary, outlining)* — 18–19

Word Skills: Homophones *(Distinguishing between homophones)* — 20

Dear Dot *(Reading comprehension, understanding words through context, making judgments)* — 21

UNIT 2   Food, Diets, Nutrition

Sensible Sam *(Interpreting a chart, understanding adverbs of frequency)* — 22

Counting Calories *(Using a chart, solving mathematical word problems)* — 23

In the Kitchen (1) *(Asking/answering questions: Are there any . . .? How many . . .? using adverbs of quantity)* — 24

In the Kitchen (2) *(Asking/answering quantity questions with non-count nouns)* — 25

Tony's Place *(Interpreting a menu, solving mathematical word problems)* — 26

Beginnings and Endings *(Understanding cause and effect, combining sentences with so and because)* — 27

Food for Your Health *(Identifying main idea and details, building vocabulary, charting information)* — 28–29

Word Skills: Antonyms *(Understanding antonyms, classifying)* — 30

Dear Dot *(Reading comprehension, understanding words through context, making judgments, writing an autobiographical paragraph)* — 31

UNIT 3 On the Job

Now, Every Day, Yesterday, Tomorrow *(Simple present and past, present and past progressive, and future form: going to)* — **32**
Work Places *(Drawing conclusions, building vocabulary)* — **33**
Application Forms *(Filling out an application form)* — **34**
Social Security *(Learning about Social Security, answering application form questions)* — **35**
Let's Go! *(Using the simple past tense, regular and irregular forms)* — **36**
Choose the Verb Form *(Comparing simple present and past, present and past progressive, future form: going to)* — **37**
I'm Busy, You're Busy *(Identifying main idea and details, building vocabulary)* — **38–39**
Word Skills: Adding "ing" *(Constructing gerunds, applying rules for spelling changes)* — **40**
Dear Dot *(Reading for details, drawing conclusions, understanding words through context, making judgments, writing directions)* — **41**

UNIT 4 Tasks and Travel

Paying Bills *(Comparing present perfect, simple past, and future form: going to)* — **42**
The Garcia Family *(Using present perfect, simple past, and future form: going to)* — **43**
Carolina's Vacation *(Using the present perfect)* — **44**
Getting There *(Interpreting a subway map, giving and following directions)* — **45**
The Declaration of Independence *(Drawing conclusions, recalling details, building vocabulary, completing an outline)* — **46–47**
Word Skills: Adding "ed" *(Forming the past tense, observing spelling changes)* — **48**
Dear Dot *(Reading for details, understanding words through context, making judgments, writing a descriptive paragraph)* — **49**

UNIT 5 What About You?

Can You? Could You? *(Using modals can/can't, could/couldn't)* — **50**
Do You Have To? *(Using have to, has to, had to)* — **51**
Have You Ever? *(Using present perfect, interviewing, writing an informative paragraph)* — **52**
Have You Seen <u>Star Wars</u>? *(Using a chart to answer questions, comparing present perfect and simple past)* — **53**
A True Genius *(Reading for details, drawing conclusions, building vocabulary, determining cause and effect)* — **54–55**
Word Skills: Synonyms *(Identifying synonyms)* — **56**
Dear Dot *(Reading for details, understanding words through context, making judgments, supporting an opinion in writing)* — **57**

UNIT 6 People, Places, and Progress

The Party *(Simple past, regular and irregular forms, reading for details, writing an autobiographical paragraph)* — **58**
A Nation of Immigrants (1) *(Interpreting bar and pie graphs, writing a paragraph)* — **59**
A Nation of Immigrants (2) *(Reading tables, using an encyclopedia, graphing statistics)* — **60**

Persons and Places *(Using adjective clauses* who *and* where, *building vocabulary, drawing conclusions)* — 61
What Did You See? *(Combining sentences with* who*)* — 62
Word Skills: Prefixes *(Understanding prefixes)* — 63
The Iron Horse *(Reading for details, building vocabulary, drawing inferences, discussing opposing viewpoints)* — 64–65
Dear Dot *(Reading for details, understanding words through context, making judgments, writing autobiographical paragraphs)* — 66

UNIT 7   Voyage to the Moon
A Trip to the Moon: 1865 *(Completing a cloze exercise)* — 67
A Trip to the Moon: 1969 *(Reading for details, reviewing verb tenses)* — 68
Word Skills: Irregular Plurals *(Constructing irregular plurals, using the dictionary to check spelling)* — 69
Our Closest Neighbor *(Drawing inferences, building vocabulary, reading for details, sequencing, researching and reporting information)* — 70–71
Library Catalog Cards *(Using the card catalog)* — 72
The Future with "Will" *(Constructing the future tense)* — 73
Dear Dot *(Reading for details, understanding words through context, making judgments, creative writing)* — 74

UNIT 8   Health and the Weather
Thank You *(Writing a thank you note)* — 75
Call the Doctor *(Building vocabulary, discussing illness and symptoms)* — 76
In the Drugstore *(Building vocabulary, discussing drug store products)* — 77
Follow the Directions *(Reading medical prescriptions and labels)* — 78
Word Skills: Categories *(Classifying, reviewing vocabulary)* — 79
Stormy Weather! *(Reading for details, building vocabulary, drawing conclusions, interpreting and writing about a weather map)* — 80–81
Dear Dot *(Reading for details, understanding words through context, making judgments, writing an autobiographical paragraph)* — 82

UNIT 9   Now and in the Past
What Did She Tell You? *(Reporting speech)* — 83
How Long? *(Contrasting present perfect continuous, present progressive, and past form:* started + *gerund)* — 84
For and Since *(Describing periods of time with* for *and* since, *using present perfect continuous)* — 85
How Long and How Many? *(Comparing present perfect continuous and present perfect)* — 86
Martha Miller *(Present perfect continous, present perfect, simple past, and* plans to/wants to*)* — 87
An Important Science *(Reading for details, drawing conclusions, understanding cause and effect, doing research and writing a short report)* — 88–89
Word Skills: Category Labels *(Classifying)* — 90
Dear Dot *(Reading for details, understanding words through context, making judgments, writing an autobiographical paragraph)* — 91

UNIT 10 Anything and Everything

Something, Anything *(Using indefinite pronouns and adjectives)*	92
I Just Ate! *(Using* just *with present perfect and simple past)*	93
Using Reference Books *(Comparing the uses of different reference books)*	94
It's Your Choice *(Reviewing present perfect and simple past)*	95
Here to Stay (1) *(Predicting outcomes, building vocabulary, sequencing, drawing inferences, researching and reporting)*	96–97
Word Skills: Analogies *(Completing analogies)*	98
Two Careers *(Interpreting a chart, reviewing verb tenses)*	99
Dear Dot *(Reading for details, understanding words through context, making judgments, writing a friendly letter)*	100

UNIT 11 Odds and Ends

Word Skills: Irregular Verbs *(Reviewing past tense irregular verbs)*	101
Crossword Puzzle *(Past tense irregular verbs)*	102
By Myself *(Reviewing subject and reflexive pronouns)*	103
Water, Water Everywhere *(Identifying main idea and details, interpreting and completing a chart)*	104
Television Tonight *(Reading a TV schedule)*	105
Here to Stay (2) *(Identifying main idea and details, building vocabulary, sequencing, drawing inferences)*	106–107
Two Couples *(Reading for details, asking/answering questions)*	108
Dear Dot *(Reading for details, understanding words through context, making judgments, writing directions)*	109

UNIT 12 Good, Better, Best

Word Skills: Adding "er" and "est" *(Forming comparatives and superlatives, observing spelling changes)*	110
Pat, June, and Alice *(Forming comparatives and superlatives)*	111
Vacation Time *(Using comparatives and superlatives)*	112
More Vacation Time *(Forming comparatives and superlatives using* more *and* the most*)*	113
Inflation *(Interpreting and drawing a line graph)*	114
Summer Jobs *(Reading and comparing "Help Wanted" ads)*	115
Fact or Opinion *(Discriminating between fact and opinion)*	116
The Sunshine State *(Reading for details, interpreting a map with product symbols)*	117
Biggest, Largest, Longest! *(Reading for details, building vocabulary, drawing conclusions, classifying)*	118–119
Dear Dot *(Reading for details, understanding words through context, making judgments, writing a description)*	120

Verb Review 121–122

End of Book Test

Completing Familiar Structures	123–125
Reading Comprehension	126–127

Skills Index 128

A Busy Morning

Side note (left margin, top): class, What does (Monica) do every morning? ("She washes her face." "She gets dressed." etc.) Remind students that verbs ending in -s, -sh, -ch and -x add the ending -es. Assign the page as independent or pair work. Correct as a class.

Side note (left margin, bottom): **Skill Objective: Reviewing present tense, third person singular** Ask a volunteer to pantomime the following morning activities: get dressed, wash your face, eat breakfast, brush your teeth, open the door, wave goodbye, close the door, walk to school. Before each action ask the

Look at the picture story of Jane's morning. Use it to answer the following questions. Use complete sentences. The first one is done for you. Use it as a model for the others.

1. Does Jane run or walk to the bathroom?

   She runs to the bathroom.

2. Does she brush her teeth or her hair?

3. Does she wash her face or her feet?

4. Does she go to the kitchen or the bedroom?

5. Does she drink coffee or tea?

6. Does she get dressed before breakfast or after breakfast?

7. Does she rush to the bus stop or to the garage?

8. Does she catch the bus or does she miss it?

Skill Sharpeners 3—Starting Out

Small Talk

A. Complete each of these sentences. This first one is done for you.

1. I'm going to the library because _I want to take out some books._
2. She has to walk to work because _____
3. The concert started late because _____
4. She didn't go to school because _____
5. The girls don't want to go to that movie because _____
6. We are driving to California because _____
7. We stopped at the supermarket because _____
8. We are going to a restaurant because _____
9. David is taking the train to Dallas because _____

B. Read the following questions. Answer each question by making a check mark in the right box under *Yes*, *No*, or *Sometimes*.

	Yes	No	Sometimes
1. Do shirts have buttons?			
2. Do shoes have zippers?			
3. Do pants have sleeves?			
4. Do pants have zippers?			
5. Do men wear blouses?			
6. Do belts go around the chest?			
7. Do hats go on people's heads?			
8. Do shirts have collars?			
9. Do skirts have hems?			
10. Do sweaters have pockets?			

Part B: Teach/review clothing vocabulary by giving directions: *If you are wearing a zipper, sit on your desk. If you are wearing more than four buttons, write your name on the board, etc.* Complete the first two items in Part B as a class, then assign the page as independent work.

Skill Objectives: Reviewing verb tenses, understanding cause and effect, building vocabulary, charting information. Cover Part A as an oral group activity. Students should be as creative as possible and think up as many different reasons as they can for each item.

Skill Sharpeners 3—Starting Out

The New Apartment

The Wang family are in their new apartment. Everyone is busy, helping to fix it up.

A. Use the Memory Bank to complete each of the following sentences. Use your dictionary if there are other words you are not sure of.

1. Mrs. Wang is painting the walls. She's using paint and a _____.
2. Lee Wang is putting a picture on the wall. He's using nails and a _____.
3. Kim is measuring for curtains. She's using a _____.
4. Mr. Wang is connecting the antenna to the TV. He's using a _____.
5. Wu Wang is installing an extension telephone. He's using a pair of _____.

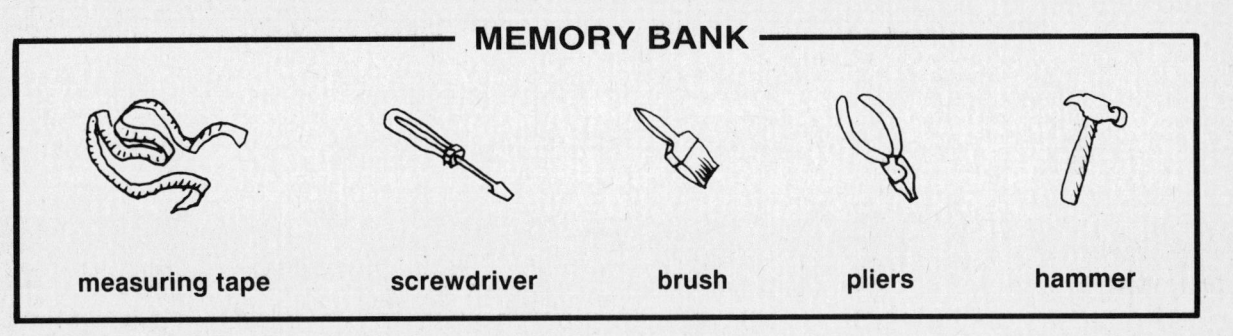

MEMORY BANK

measuring tape   screwdriver   brush   pliers   hammer

B. Now look at the pictures below. Each picture illustrates one of the sentences about the Wang family. Put a number under each picture to show the sentence that it goes with.

____ ____ ____ ____ ____

C. Write about the Wangs' apartment. What color are the walls? What is the picture that Lee is putting on the wall? What will the curtains be like? Write as many things as you can about the apartment. Use more paper if you need to.

Skill Sharpeners 3—Starting Out

Two Hundred Years of American History

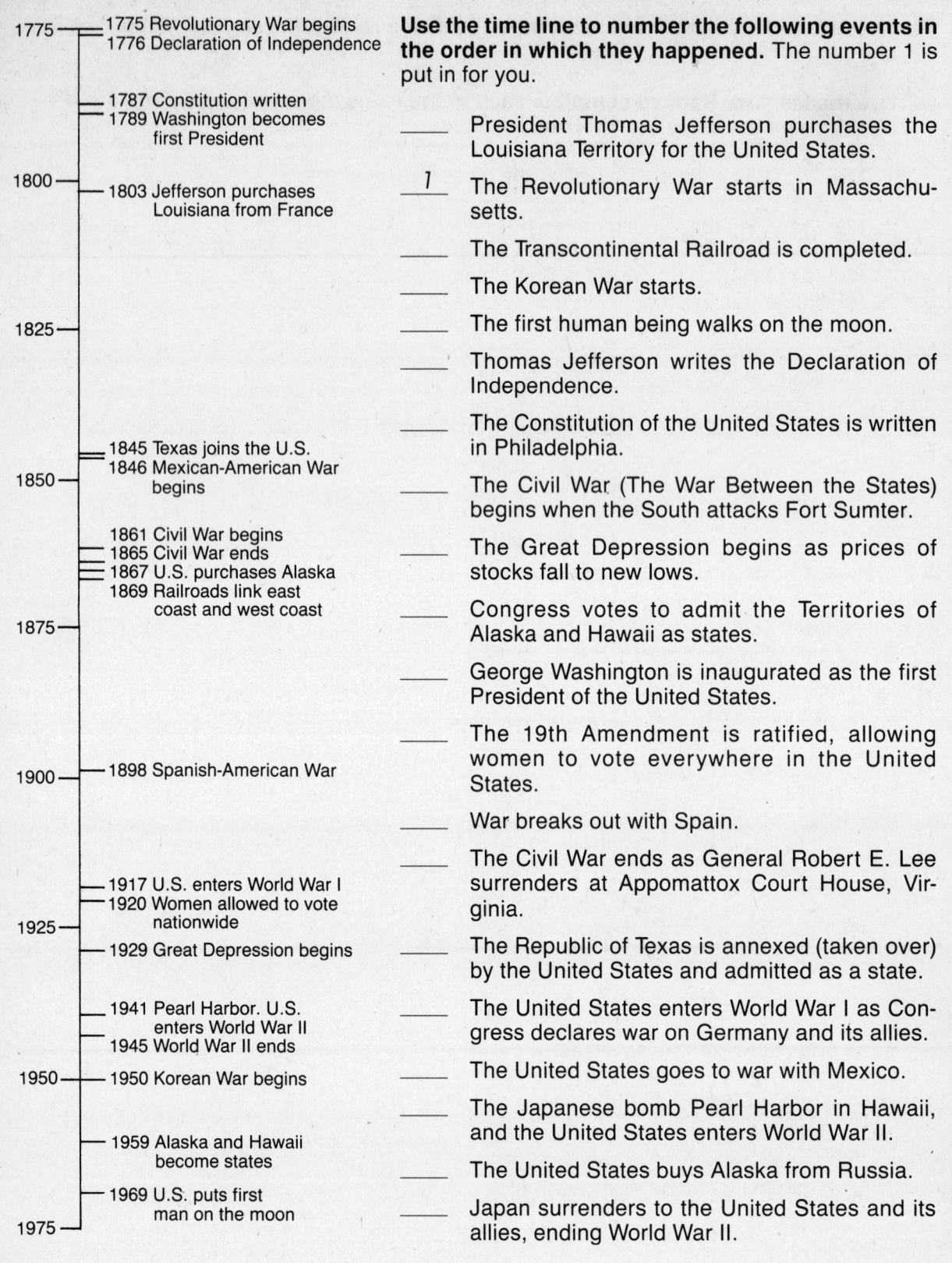

Timeline:

- 1775 Revolutionary War begins
- 1776 Declaration of Independence
- 1787 Constitution written
- 1789 Washington becomes first President
- 1803 Jefferson purchases Louisiana from France
- 1845 Texas joins the U.S.
- 1846 Mexican-American War begins
- 1861 Civil War begins
- 1865 Civil War ends
- 1867 U.S. purchases Alaska
- 1869 Railroads link east coast and west coast
- 1898 Spanish-American War
- 1917 U.S. enters World War I
- 1920 Women allowed to vote nationwide
- 1929 Great Depression begins
- 1941 Pearl Harbor. U.S. enters World War II
- 1945 World War II ends
- 1950 Korean War begins
- 1959 Alaska and Hawaii become states
- 1969 U.S. puts first man on the moon

Use the time line to number the following events in the order in which they happened. The number 1 is put in for you.

___ President Thomas Jefferson purchases the Louisiana Territory for the United States.

_1_ The Revolutionary War starts in Massachusetts.

___ The Transcontinental Railroad is completed.

___ The Korean War starts.

___ The first human being walks on the moon.

___ Thomas Jefferson writes the Declaration of Independence.

___ The Constitution of the United States is written in Philadelphia.

___ The Civil War (The War Between the States) begins when the South attacks Fort Sumter.

___ The Great Depression begins as prices of stocks fall to new lows.

___ Congress votes to admit the Territories of Alaska and Hawaii as states.

___ George Washington is inaugurated as the first President of the United States.

___ The 19th Amendment is ratified, allowing women to vote everywhere in the United States.

___ War breaks out with Spain.

___ The Civil War ends as General Robert E. Lee surrenders at Appomattox Court House, Virginia.

___ The Republic of Texas is annexed (taken over) by the United States and admitted as a state.

___ The United States enters World War I as Congress declares war on Germany and its allies.

___ The United States goes to war with Mexico.

___ The Japanese bomb Pearl Harbor in Hawaii, and the United States enters World War II.

___ The United States buys Alaska from Russia.

___ Japan surrenders to the United States and its allies, ending World War II.

Alaska and Hawaii become states? Have students locate the four states on a map. Help students locate and number the sentences that tell about the first few events on the time line, then assign the page for independent or pair work. Correct and discuss as a class.

Skill Objectives: Interpreting a time line, identifying main idea, sequencing

Allow time for students to read the time line, then ask, When did Jefferson buy Louisiana from France? When did Texas join the U.S.? When did

Skill Sharpeners 3—Starting Out

Affirmative and Negative

A. Change the following statements from affirmative to negative. The first one is done for you.

1. Jan speaks English very well.   *Jan doesn't speak English very well.*
2. The bus arrived on time.   _____
3. Paul is leaving in the morning.   _____
4. They take the subway to work.   _____
5. My father has two jobs.   _____
6. The stores were closed on Sunday.   _____
7. I do my homework every night.   _____
8. The teacher came late.   _____
9. This typewriter works well.   _____
10. Mr. Jones cut his finger.   _____
11. Henry likes to play volleyball.   _____
12. It rains in Los Angeles a lot.   _____

B. Change the following sentences to questions. The first one is done for you.

1. They went to a Chinese Restaurant.
   Where *did they go* _____?
2. Mrs. Friedman works 12 hours a day.
   How many _____?
3. The teacher told us to study more.
   What _____?
4. She's staying in Miami for two weeks.
   How long _____?
5. Fred plays soccer every Saturday.
   When _____?
6. President Reagan makes $200,000 a year.
   How much _____?
7. She's crying because she's sad.
   Why _____?
8. She teaches at Central Junior High School.
   Where _____?

Skill Sharpeners 3—Starting Out

Likes and Dislikes

Most people like to do some things and do not like to do others. Look at the pictures. Then write what the persons or animals like to do and what they don't like to do. The first one is done for you. Use it as a model for the others.

1. *Samir likes playing baseball, but he doesn't like studying history.*

2. *Carolina*

3. *Binh*

4. *Ed and Al*

5. *My cat*

6. *They*

7. *Elena*

Skill Objective: Using like(s), doesn't/don't like plus gerund. Give several statements of likes/dislikes: *I like skiing, but I don't like skating. I like eating, but I don't like gaining weight.* Ask students, "How about you?" After four or five have volunteered, ask their classmates to recall their statements. *Alicia likes playing with babies, but she doesn't like changing them.* If students use the infinitive verb instead of the gerund ("likes to play"), praise the sentence as correct, and encourage students to use both forms for variety. Assign the page for written work.

14   Skill Sharpeners 3—Unit 1

Yes or No?

A. Answer each of the questions. Use short answers and pay attention to the tense. Look at the three examples. Use them as models for your own answers.

Example A. Can you speak French?   *No, I can't.*
Example B. Do you like to play volleyball?   *Yes, I do.*
Example C. Did you do your homework?   *Yes, I did.*

1. Does your teacher live in New York?   _____
2. Was yesterday Monday?   _____
3. Did you watch TV last night?   _____
4. Is the weather hot today?   _____
5. Can you water ski?   _____
6. Do you have two brothers?   _____
7. Does your father work at a bank?   _____
8. Were your friends busy yesterday?   _____
9. Are there any computers in your school?   _____
10. Are you going to the movies tonight?   _____
11. Do you like ice cream?   _____
12. Did it rain yesterday?   _____

B. Now write questions for the answers. The first one is done for you.

1. *Are you eighteen* ? No, I'm not. I'm fifteen.
2. _____? No, I don't. I like to ski.
3. _____? No, she didn't. She went to the concert.
4. _____? No, they can't. They can play the violin.
5. _____? No, he isn't. He's short.
6. _____? No, he doesn't. He likes rock music.
7. _____? No, it isn't. It's sunny.
8. _____? No, they aren't. They're going to Illinois.
9. _____? No, he wasn't. He was wearing a red tie.
10. _____? No, I wasn't. I was sick.

Skill Objective: Asking/answering questions: Can...? Do/Does/Did...? Is/Are/Was/Were...? Write on the board: Can you? Do you? Does your...? Did you? Are you? Is your...? Were you? Was your...? Ask questions using these forms. "Does your father smoke?" "Yes, he does./No, he doesn't." Form a chain conversation. The first student asks the person on her/his right a question, using one of the forms. That student answers, then questions the next person. Afterwards, assign the page as written work.

Skill Sharpeners 3—Unit 1

Choose the Best Word

Circle the best answer. The first one is done for you.

1. I didn't see you last night. Where [was / **were**] you?
2. Robert can't [**find** / found] his shoes.
3. Does Kit Ming [takes / **take**] the bus to school?
4. Everyone [**was** / were] dancing and singing at the party.
5. I [**went** / go] to the dentist yesterday.
6. Did you [**like** / liked] the movie?
7. Jim is [**doing** / does] his homework now.
8. Are you [rent / **renting**] an apartment?
9. [**Do** / Are] you play volleyball?
10. I'm [have / **having**] a party tonight. Can you come?
11. Ronald likes [ride / **riding**] his bicycle to school.
12. [**Was** / Were] Minh in class yesterday?
13. Maria [**writes** / writing] to her grandmother every month.
14. [Was / **Were**] the teachers at a meeting yesterday?
15. The bus [leaving / **leaves**] at ten o'clock.
16. George didn't [washed / **wash**] the dishes.

Skill Objective: Choosing the correct verb tense and form: simple present and past, present and past progressive. This page may be used as a quick evaluation of the students' ability to distinguish and use the four verb tenses. Do the first example as a group activity, then assign the page as independent work. Students who find the page difficult should be grouped for reteaching. Analyze the type of mistakes being made and provide additional practice in these skills.

Skill Sharpeners 3—Unit 1

Alternative Word Meanings

The dictionary often lists several meanings for one word. Read the following dictionary entries. **Decide which meaning of the word is being used in each sentence. Write the number of that definition in front of the sentence.** The first one is done for you.

run
1. to move rapidly
2. to take part in a race or election
3. to manage, be in charge of
4. to operate, work or move

_3_ My father runs the supermarket on 12th Street.
___ Paul Lopez is going to run for class president.
___ There's my bus. I've got to run!
___ My car runs best on premium gas.

note
1. a musical sound
2. a short letter
3. reputation or fame

___ The song ended on a sweet note.
___ Jason's mother wrote his teacher a note.
___ Henry Larkin is a musician of some note.

fly
1. to move through the air with wings
2. to pass quickly
3. to wave in the air
4. to travel by aircraft

___ Paul Peterson, the reporter, has to fly to the West Coast often.
___ Most birds fly south for the winter.
___ Time does fly when you're having fun.
___ Fly the flag proudly, boys.

poor
1. needy, having too little money
2. unhappy, deserving pity
3. unsatisfactory, not good

___ Your poor performance on this test shows that you didn't study.
___ There are many poor people in this city.
___ Look at that poor, wet cat.

carry
1. to pick up and bring
2. to win
3. to hold up, support
4. to have for sale

___ Jose, can you carry these books downstairs, please?
___ This little wagon can carry over 100 pounds.
___ Did the Democrats carry this state in the last election?
___ This store doesn't carry calendars.

Skill Sharpeners 3—Unit 1

More Than a Name

A. Read the story quickly to get a general idea of the subject. Then look at the Vocabulary Highlights. These words are underlined in the story. Be sure you understand the meaning of each word as it is used in the story. Check in the dictionary if you are unsure. Remember, some words have more than one meaning. Write down the meanings of the words that are new to you.

Vocabulary Highlights

famous	continued
personalities	talented
ended	foreign
tobacco	architecture
mules	designed

B. Now read the story again. Use the dictionary if there are other words you do not understand.

Our First Three Presidents

Many times when people study history, they learn a few facts about the famous names that they see in their text books, but they don't learn about the personalities of these famous people. For example, every student of American history knows that George Washington, John Adams, and Thomas Jefferson were the first three Presidents of the United States, but what else do they know about these interesting men?

George Washington was a quiet man. He liked to hunt and fish. He liked to give parties, but he also liked to go to bed early. His parties always ended at 9:00. After George Washington was President, he lived on his farm. He liked planting tobacco and raising mules.

John Adams was a bright and serious man. He liked to study law and history. After he was President, he returned to his home in Massachusetts. He continued to study. He liked to write about politics. He wrote many famous letters to the next president, Thomas Jefferson.

Thomas Jefferson, the third president, was a very talented man. In some ways he was like George Washington. He liked living on a farm, and he liked riding horses and hunting. Thomas Jefferson had other interests, too. He liked to play the violin, and he liked to sing. He liked speaking foreign languages, and he learned Latin, Greek, Italian, French, and Spanish. After Jefferson was President, he returned to one of his other interests, architecture. He designed the buildings for the University of Virginia.

Now you know a little more about the first three Presidents. When you are studying history, remember that the people in the books are more than names. Don't be afraid to go to the library and find out more about their personalities.

(Go on to the next page.)

C. **What is the main idea of the story? Circle the best answer.**

1. Washington, Adams, and Jefferson were our first three Presidents.
2. Washington, Adams, and Jefferson had many different interests.
3. Washington, Adams, and Jefferson went home after they were President.
4. Washington, Adams, and Jefferson are famous names.

D. **Use a word from the Vocabulary Highlights to complete each of these sentences.**

1. Pierre can sing, dance, and play the piano. He's very _____.
2. Everybody knows James Bond; he's a _____ character.
3. The party started at 8:00 and _____ at 12:30.
4. I don't understand these words; they are in a _____ language.
5. The music stopped for a moment and then _____.

E. **Answer these questions on another piece of paper.**

1. Who were the first three Presidents of the United States?
2. Why did George Washington's parties end at 9:00?
3. What did George Washington like to do on his farm?
4. What did John Adams like to study?
5. Where did John Adams live?
6. How were Thomas Jefferson and George Washington alike?
7. What foreign languages did Thomas Jefferson learn?
8. What did Thomas Jefferson do at the University of Virginia?

F. **Complete this outline of the story by filling in details.**

A. Things George Washington liked to do.

1. _____
2. _____
3. _____

B. Things John Adams liked to do.

1. _____
2. _____
3. _____

C. Things Thomas Jefferson liked to do.

1. _____
2. _____
3. _____

Skill Sharpeners 3—Unit 1

Word Skills: Homophones

Some words in English sound exactly alike but have different spellings and meanings. These words are called *homophones*. Here are some examples of homophones.

He ate eight eggs.   **She rode down the road.**   **My son is playing in the sun.**

Complete the following sentences. Use the words in the Memory Bank. Your dictionary will help you choose the correct homophone. The first one is done for you.

1. He is a vegetarian; he doesn't eat ____meat____.
2. Mei Lee knows how to _____ her own clothes.
3. There are sixty minutes in one _____.
4. Yesterday, there was a big _____ at the department store.
5. The Sampsons are going to visit _____ daughter.
6. Sonia traveled to California by _____.
7. Hanibal is shopping; he wants a new _____ of shoes.
8. Everyone wants to go _____ the movies tonight.
9. Speak a little louder please. I can't _____ you.
10. Please _____ here until the boys come out.
11. The Turners are going to _____ a new car.
12. Walk to the end of the street and turn _____.
13. The girls _____ the answer, but I don't.
14. Rita received three letters in today's _____.
15. The students stayed in New York last _____.
16. James punched Peter in the _____ this morning.

MEMORY BANK

by, buy, bye	meat, meet	plane, plain	their, there, they're
eye, I	no, know	right, write	to, two, too
here, hear	our, hour	sail, sale	wait, weight
mail, male	pear, pair	so, sew	weak, week

Skill Objective: Distinguishing between homophones
Review the definition of homophones and go over the three illustrated examples with the class. Complete several items as a group, then assign the page as independent work. Extension Activity: Encourage students to use the homophones in the Memory Bank to write sentences similar to the three at the top of this page. Each sentence should contain two or more homophones. Example: *I feel weak this week.*

Skill Sharpeners 3—Unit 1

Dear Dot

Dear Dot—

Last week I was playing tennis with my boyfriend, Jimmy. We played three matches, and I was the winner every time. Jimmy was very angry. He said he was never going to play tennis with me again. I like tennis because it is such good exercise. How can I convince Jimmy to continue playing tennis with me?

Chrissy

1. When were Chrissy and Jimmy playing tennis? _____
   _____

2. How many matches did they play? _____

3. Why do you think Jimmy was angry? _____
   _____

4. What did Jimmy say to Chrissy? _____
   _____

5. Why does Chrissy like to play tennis? _____
   _____

6. What does the word *convince* mean as used in this letter? Circle the best answer.

    a. beat   b. bother   c. bring   d. talk into

7. What is your advice to Chrissy? Discuss your answer in class. Then read Dot's answer, and tell why you agree or disagree. Dot's advice is below.

Dear Chrissy—

Try talking to Jimmy. Does he really want you not to play just as well as you can? Does he really think that men have to be superior to women? If he does (or you think that he does) find another tennis partner. And think about Jimmy's attitude before you get too serious with him.

Dot

Skill Objectives: Reading comprehension, understanding words through context, making judgments

Have students read the letter and answer the questions independently. If you wish, have students write their advice to Chrissy on a separate piece of paper. Correct the page as a class, then have students compare and discuss their own advice and Dot's reply. You may want to raise these questions for discussion: "Why do you think Jimmy got angry?" "How do you think Jimmy would have acted if he had lost the match to another boy?"

Skill Sharpeners 3—Unit 1   21

Sensible Sam

Sam tries to be sensible about eating. This chart shows some of the things he does. **Look at the chart, and then follow the instructions below it.**

	Always	Usually	Sometimes	Seldom	Never
1. Eats a good breakfast	X				
2. Has a bowl of cereal with fruit		X			
3. Has two scrambled eggs			X		
4. Drinks cola for breakfast					X
5. Brings lunch to school			X		
6. Buys lunch in cafeteria			X		
7. Skips lunch				X	
8. Eats dinner with his family at 6:30	X				
9. Helps in the kitchen after dinner		X			

A. Use the chart to write about Sam. The first two sentences are done for you.

Sam tries to eat sensibly. He always eats a good breakfast.

_____
_____
_____
_____
_____

B. Now write about you. Use the verbs in Part A.

_____
_____
_____
_____
_____

22

Skill Sharpeners 3—Unit 2

Counting Calories

A calorie is a measure of the energy you get from food. If the food you eat supplies more calories than you use up, you gain weight. If it supplies fewer calories than you use up, you lose weight. **Look at these two diets. One is for a person who is trying to lose weight. Can you tell which one it is? Use the two diets to complete the sentences under them.**

BREAKFAST	Calories	BREAKFAST	Calories
orange juice (½ cup)	55	orange juice (1 cup)	110
boiled egg	80	1 fried egg	95
whole wheat toast	55	2 slices bacon	90
1 pat butter	50	coffee	
cup coffee/skim milk	0	1 tsp. whole milk	20
total	240	1 tsp. sugar	18
		total	333
LUNCH		LUNCH	
tomato juice (½ cup)	25	hamburger (4 oz.)	320
tuna salad (½ cup)	180	roll	120
1 slice Syrian bread	80	1 can of cola (12 oz.)	150
1 medium apple	75	French fries (1 cup)	570
1 can of diet cola (12 oz.)	1	1 banana	95
total	361	total	1255
DINNER		DINNER	
broiled chicken (6 oz.)	320	fried chicken (6 oz.)	520
½ cup peas	60	1 boiled potato	125
½ cup squash	50	1 cup peas	120
1 cup skim milk	75	1 slice French bread	120
1 pat butter	50	1 cup squash	100
total	555	3 pats butter	150
		1 cup whole milk	175
		1 cup gelatin dessert	140
		total	1450
grand total	1156	grand total	3038

1. One slice of bacon has _____ calories.

2. Syrian bread has (more, fewer) calories than whole wheat bread. (Circle one.)

3. There are _____ more calories in a cup of milk than in a cup of skim milk.

4. Six ounces of broiled chicken has _____ fewer calories than six ounces of fried chicken.

5. There are _____ calories in one cup of tomato juice.

6. An apple has _____ fewer calories than a banana.

7. A hamburger, including the roll, has _____ calories.

8. A can of regular cola has _____ more calories than a can of diet cola.

9. A fried egg has _____ more calories than a boiled egg.

10. Two bananas have _____ calories.

Skill Sharpeners 3—Unit 2

Skill Objectives: Using a chart, solving math word problems
Some students will be able to complete this page independently, others will need your continued guidance. For each question ask, *What information can you find on the chart? What is the question you have to answer? How can you use the information to get the answer?* **Extension Activity:** As a class, examine the meals on the chart to see if each contains food from the necessary nutritional groups: A. protein (meat, fish, dairy, eggs, nuts); B. fruits and vegetables; C. bread and cereals.

In the Kitchen (1)

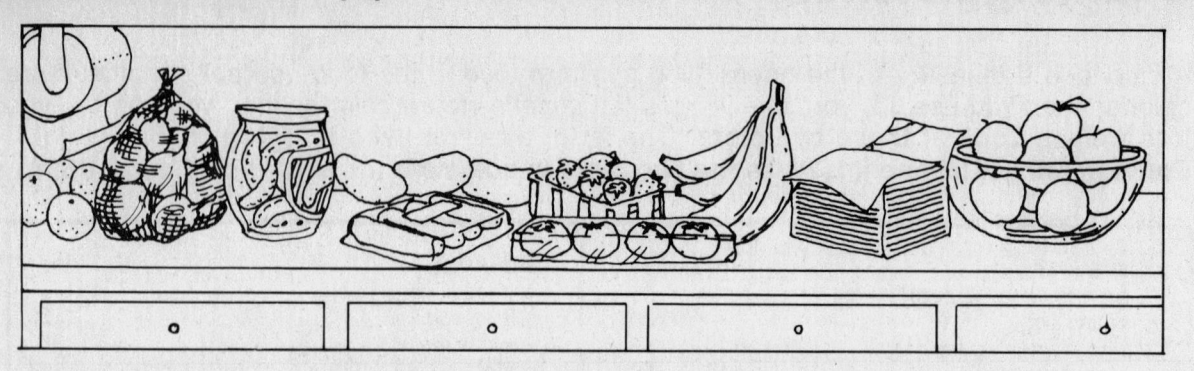

Look at the picture of the kitchen counter. Use it to answer the questions. Where the answers are given, make up questions to go with them. The first three are done for you.

1. Are there any apples in this kitchen? *Yes, there are many.*
2. Are there any pears in this kitchen? *No, there aren't any. (or "are none")*
3. Are there any oranges in this kitchen? *Yes, there are some. (or "a few")*
4. Are there any cookies in this kitchen? _____
5. Are there any napkins? _____
6. Are there any bananas? _____
7. Are there any eggs? _____
8. Are there any lemons? _____
9. Are there any sandwiches for lunch? _____
10. Are there any pickles? _____
11. Are there any tomatoes? _____
12. Are there any lamb chops? _____
13. Are there any paper towels? _____
14. _____? Yes, there are a few.
15. _____? No, there aren't any.
16. _____? Yes, there are many.
17. _____? No, there are none.
18. How many hot dog rolls are there? _____
19. How many hot dogs are there? _____
20. How many potatoes are there? _____

Skill Objectives: Asking/answering questions, *Are there any...? How many...?*, using adverbs of quantity. Be sure students understand that the questions can also be answered with an exact number. After sufficient oral practice, assign the page for independent work.

Write on the board: *Are there any...? How many... are there?* many, quite a few, some, a few, none/aren't any. Teach/review the adverbs of quantity. Have students use the two question forms to ask each other about the number or items in the picture.

24   Skill Sharpeners 3—Unit 2

In the Kitchen (2)

Mr. Garcia has come back from the supermarket and is putting away the things he bought. **Look at the picture and answer the questions about Mr. Garcia's groceries. Where the answers are given, make up questions to go with them.** The first three are done for you.

1. Is there any corn? *Yes, there is a lot.*
2. Is there any tuna fish? *No, there isn't any. (or "is none")*
3. Is there any lettuce? *Yes, there is some. (or "a little")*
4. Is there any orange juice? _____
5. Is there any sugar? _____
6. Is there any soap? _____
7. Is there any bread? _____
8. Is there any bacon? _____
9. Is there any ketchup? _____
10. Is there any salad oil? _____
11. Is there any cereal? _____
12. Is there any toothpaste? _____
13. Is there any cake? _____
14. _____? Yes, there is some.
15. _____? No, there isn't any.
16. How much soup is there? _____
17. How much rice is there? _____
18. How much butter is there? _____

Skill Objective: Asking/answering quantity questions with non-count nouns. Write: *Is there any . . . ? How much . . . is there?* Teach the adverbs of quantity: *a lot, quite a lot, some, a little, none/isn't any*. Have students ask/answer questions about the picture. Draw a ¼-filled ketchup bottle, a stack of soap, two eggs and ten oranges. Ask, *How much ketchup/soap is there? How many eggs/oranges are there?* (*a little, a lot; a few, many*) Note the different adverbs used with count vs. non-count nouns.

Skill Sharpeners 3—Unit 2

25

Tony's Place

```
         OPEN 7 DAYS   6 A.M.–11 P.M. MON.–FRI.   9 A.M.–11 P.M. SAT. & SUN.
                                    –SUBS–
                  SM.   LG.                    SM.   LG.                    SM.   LG.
Cold Cuts         2.00  2.40   Tuna Salad      2.00  2.40   Sliced Turkey   2.00  2.40
Roast Beef        2.40  2.70   Bologna-Cheese  1.90  2.30   Salami-Cheese   2.00  2.40
Ham & Cheese      2.00  2.40   Crabmeat        2.35  2.95   Chicken Salad   2.00  2.40

                                –Try the hot ones–
Steak             2.10  2.45   Sausage             2.00  2.40   Western       2.00  2.40
Steak-Peppers     2.25  2.60   Sausage & Meatball  2.00  2.40   Ham-Egg       2.00  2.40
Steak-Onions      2.25  2.60   Veal Cutlet         2.40  2.70   Hamburger     1.80  2.30
Meatball          2.00  2.40   Pastromi            2.00  2.40   Cheeseburger  1.95  2.45

                             –PIZZA WITH PIZZAZZ–
Cheese       2.25   Salami      2.75   Ham             2.25
Onion        2.25   Pepperoni   2.75   Bacon           2.75
Pepper       2.55   Anchovie    2.75   Any 2 Combo     3.10
Mushroom     2.75   Hamburg     2.75   Any 3 Combo     3.25
Sausage      2.75   Linguica    2.75   Any 4 Combo     3.50
                      Buy 3 Pizzas—Get One Free
             Pizza Served Mon.–Thurs. 5–11 P.M.   Fri.–Sun. 4–11 P.M.

         BEVERAGES                              SIDE SPECIALS
Milk     .40            Coffee   .30  .40    French Fries      Onion Rings
Juice    .40            Tea      .30  .40    .60  .85  1.20    .65  .95  1.30
Soda     .35  .45  .50  Sanka    .35  .45
```

Look at Tony's menu. Use your dictionary for words you do not know. (You may not find *sub*. It is a kind of sandwich made with a loaf of French bread that is split from end to end, and it has different names in different parts of the country.) **Now answer the questions about Tony's menu. Use short answers.**

1. Why are there two prices for each sub? _____

2. How much is a large steak and onion sub? _____

3. How much is a small cold cut sub with a small order of French fries? _____

4. Do they probably sell cola in Tony's Place? _____

5. "Combo" stands for combination. What do you think a combo pizza is? _____
   _____

6. How much is one pizza with onions, peppers, sausage, and pepperoni? _____

7. Is Tony's Place open every day? _____

8. Merle bought four pizzas. How many did she have to pay for? _____

9. Can you buy a pizza for lunch at Tony's? _____

10. Binh wants to buy a pizza with mushrooms and onions. How much will he have to pay for it? _____

Beginnings and Endings

Find the right ending for each sentence, and write its letter in the blank. Each letter may be used only once. The first one is done for you.

1. Lisa always studies, so __j__
2. Pablo always gets up late, so ____
3. Chang never eats breakfast, so ____
4. Mr. Watson seldom drives his car, so ____
5. The baby usually sleeps in the afternoon, so ____
6. Luis is always smiling, so ____
7. Peter frequently drives fast, so ____
8. Dulce doesn't know what's happening in the world because ____
9. My little sister sometimes gets sick because ____
10. Wanda's boss is very angry at her because ____
11. Jill doesn't buy much at the cafeteria because ____
12. All the students want Mei Ling on their team because ____
13. Mr. Fell's students study hard every Thursday night because ____
14. Because it usually rains on weekends, ____
15. Because that store closes at 5:00, ____
16. Because Michael almost never eats sugar, ____
17. Because my uncle seldom writes letters, ____
18. Because English often is confusing, ____
19. Because the students sometimes are noisy, ____
20. Because my father always plays chess at my uncle's house on Friday night, ____

a. he's very hungry at lunch.
b. she always hits a home run.
c. we stay inside on Saturday and Sunday.
d. we have to be quiet when we get home from school.
e. the teacher has to tell them to be quiet.
f. he get a lot of tickets.
g. his teeth are in good condition.
h. she eats too much.
i. you have to shop early.
j. she gets good grades on her report card.
k. we call him on the phone every month.
l. she usually brings her lunch.
m. people are glad to see him.
n. he comes home late.
o. he often misses his first class.
p. you have to study it very carefully.
q. she almost never watches the news on TV.
r. he gives tests on Friday.
s. it is in good condition.
t. she often misses work.

Skill Sharpeners 3—Unit 2

Food for Your Health

A. Read the story quickly to get a general idea of the subject. Then look at the Vocabulary Highlights. These words are underlined in the story. Be sure you understand the meaning of each word as it is used in the story. Check in the dictionary if you are unsure. Remember, some words have more than one meaning. Write down the meanings of the words that are new to you.

Vocabulary Highlights

necessary	poultry
health	digest
major	prevent
specific	bleeding

B. Now read the story again. Use the dictionary if there are other words you do not understand.

Vitamins

Vitamins are <u>necessary</u> for good <u>health</u>. We get vitamins from the foods that we eat. There are about ten <u>major</u> vitamins. Each vitamin has a <u>specific</u> job to do in the body. Read about vitamins below.

- Vitamin A—Vitamin A comes from green and yellow vegetables. It is also in milk and egg yolks. Vitamin A is necessary for night vision, seeing in the dark.

- Vitamin B_1—Vitamin B_1 comes from fish, brown rice, and <u>poultry</u>. It is also in most meats and nuts. The job of vitamin B_1 is to build the blood and help the body <u>digest</u> food.

- Vitamin B_{12}—Vitamin B_{12} comes from cheese, fish, and milk. The job of vitamin B_{12} is to build up the red blood cells and to keep the body's nervous system healthy.

- Vitamin C—Vitamin C comes from citrus fruits such as oranges and grapefruit and other fruits such as strawberries. It is also in green peppers. Vitamin C is important in building bones and teeth, and some people say it helps to <u>prevent</u> colds.

- Vitamin D—Vitamin D comes from egg yolks. In the United States, the dairy industry also adds it to milk. People also get vitamin D from sunlight. Vitamin D is important for building strong bones.

- Vitamin E—Vitamin E comes from dark green vegetables such as spinach. It is also found in eggs and liver. Vitamin E is important in reproduction and muscle development.

- Vitamin K—Vitamin K comes from green leafy vegetables and yogurt. Its job is to help the blood to clot. Without vitamin K, cuts and scrapes keep <u>bleeding</u>. Vitamin K helps the cut to close. It keeps the body from losing too much blood.

(Go on to the next page.)

Skill Sharpeners 3—Unit 2

C. Circle the answer that best completes the sentence.

Vitamins are necessary for good health because

a. they are found in certain foods.
b. they have important jobs to do in the body.
c. there are ten major vitamins.
d. they are chemical substances.

D. Use a word from the Vocabulary Highlights to complete each of these sentences.

1. Quick, get a bandage! Diana is _____.

2. Smoking is the _____ cause of lung cancer.

3. I don't understand your problem; please be more _____.

4. Don't let accidents happen; try to _____ them.

5. Most people agree that you can't be happy without your _____.

E. Use separate paper to write answers to these questions. (Number your answers to match the questions.)

1. What are three vitamins that come from green vegetables?
2. What vitamin does brown rice contain?
3. What vitamin do both egg yolks and sunlight provide?
4. What vitamin helps keep the nervous system healthy?
5. What vitamin helps blood to clot?
6. What does "clot" mean?
7. What fruits give us a good supply of vitamin C?
8. What foods give us a good supply of vitamin E?
9. What vitamin helps the body to digest food?
10. What is night vision?

F. Look at the list of foods below. They have lots of vitamins. Are they part of your diet (what you eat)? Complete the chart by checking if you eat *lots of*, *some*, or *none* of each of the foods on the list.

	Lots of	Some	None
liver			
milk			
eggs			
fish			
nuts			
poultry			
green vegetables			
fruits			
rice			

Skill Sharpeners 3—Unit 2

Word Skills: Antonyms

Antonyms are words that are opposite in meaning. *High* and *low* are antonyms because high is the opposite of low. Not every word has an antonym, but many do. Here are some common English antonyms. **Read the list and then answer the questions under it.**

always/never	clean/dirty	right/left	before/after
often/seldom	open/close	in/out	big/little
question/answer	dead/alive	start/finish	day/night
arrive/leave	east/west	stop/go	near/far
awake/asleep	first/last	on/off	hello/goodbye
begin/end	front/back	up/down	hot/cold
buy/sell	love/hate		

1. Which antonym pair describes what you do in a store? _____
2. Which antonym pair describes directions on a map? _____
3. Which antonym pair describes a race? _____
4. Which antonym pair describes a red light and a green light? _____
5. Which antonym pair describes strong emotions? _____
6. Which antonym pair describes the weather? _____
7. Which antonym pair describes an elephant and an ant? _____
8. Which antonym pair describes sunlight and moonlight? _____
9. Which antonym pair describes a school test? _____
10. Which antonym pair describes out of bed or in bed? _____
11. Which antonym pair describes distances? _____
12. Which antonym pair describes car turn signals? _____
13. Which antonym pair describes stairways? _____
14. Which antonym pair describes a fast conversation? _____
15. Which antonym pair describes an electrical appliance? _____
16. Which antonym pair describes what a train does? _____
17. Which antonym pair describes the two covers of a book? _____
18. Which antonym pair describes what you do to a door? _____

Skill Objectives: Understanding antonyms, classifying
Say the following words, and have the class name the opposites: yes, fat, early, young, win, empty, fast, wet, happy, summer, wonderful, tall, pretty. Assign the page as independent work. Discuss the answers as a class.

Dear Dot

Dear Dot—

My son, Ronald, never goes out. He comes home from school and changes his clothes, and then he practices the piano. He plays for hours. After dinner he does his homework, and then he goes right back to his music. He doesn't have any friends. He never watches TV, and he never goes to the movies. Is he all right? I worry about him.

Concerned Mother

1. What does Ronald do after he changes his clothes? _____

2. What does Ronald do when he isn't playing the piano? _____

3. Is Ronald a popular person? _____

4. What do you think Concerned Mother wants Ronald to do? _____

5. What is the best meaning of *concerned,* as used in this letter? Circle your answer.

   a. late   b. worried   c. strong   d. angry

6. What is your advice to Concerned Mother? Discuss your answer in class. Then read Dot's answer and tell why you agree or disagree. Dot's advice is below.

Dear Mom—

It's easy to understand why you are concerned about Ronald. I agree that he doesn't behave the way most boys of his age do. He is completely involved in music and his own small world. However, if he wants to make his living as a musician, he needs to practice, practice, and practice. You can't and shouldn't try to force a social life on him (or on anyone). What you can do is encourage him, show your interest, and be ready to listen if he wants to share his thoughts and concerns. If you just want him to go out once in a while, why not get tickets to a concert or musical show and take him out as a special treat. But be sure it's his kind of music!

Dot

Write About It

On your paper, write a paragraph describing your typical day. Tell what you do from the time you get up until you go to bed.

Skill Sharpeners 3—Unit 2

Now, Every Day, Yesterday, Tomorrow

Look at the example (*watch*). Use this as a model to fill in the four sentences for each of the other verbs. Use the pronoun (*she, they, you, I*) given next to the picture.

Example: **watch**

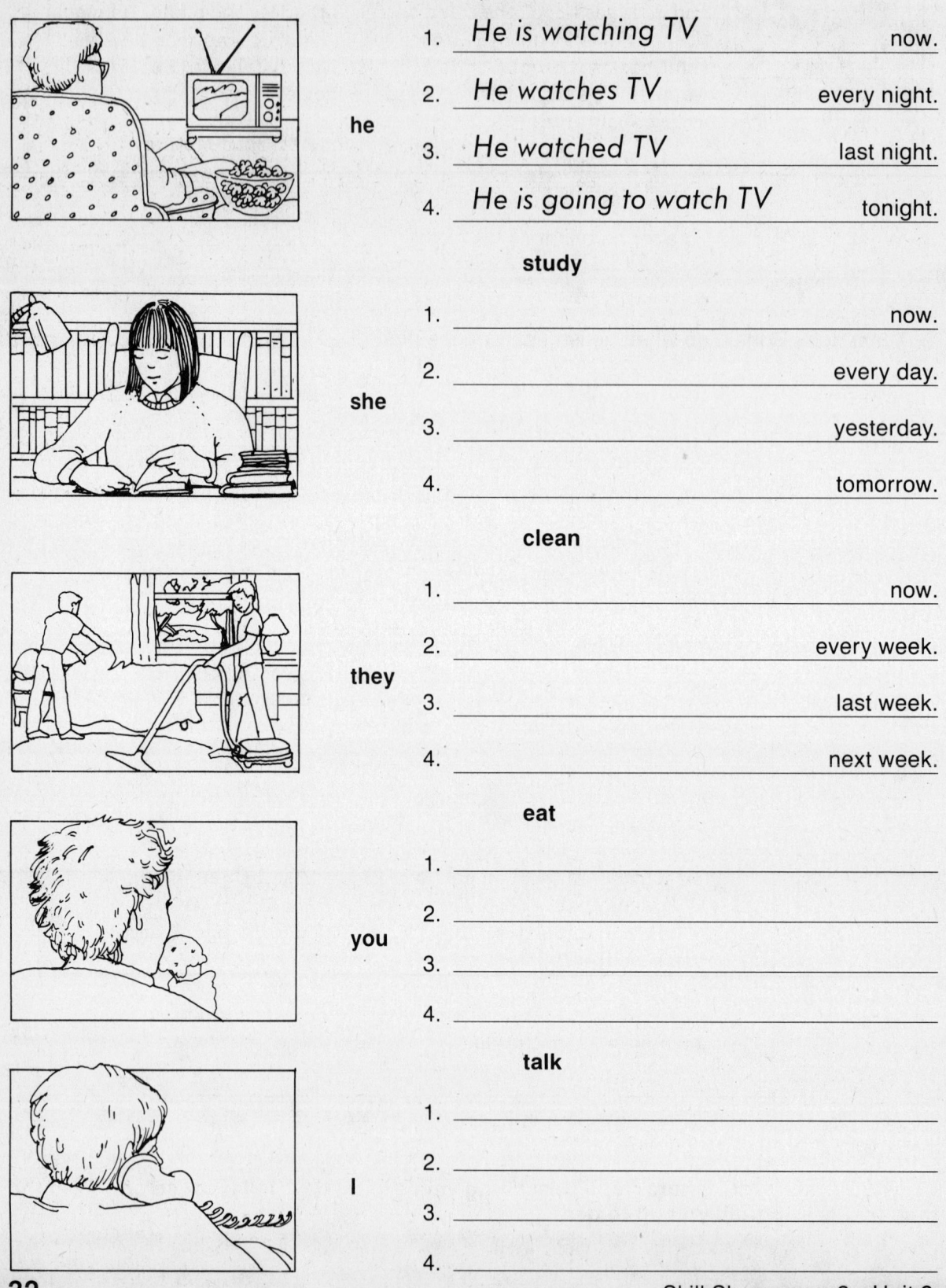

he
1. *He is watching TV* now.
2. *He watches TV* every night.
3. *He watched TV* last night.
4. *He is going to watch TV* tonight.

study

she
1. _____ now.
2. _____ every day.
3. _____ yesterday.
4. _____ tomorrow.

clean

they
1. _____ now.
2. _____ every week.
3. _____ last week.
4. _____ next week.

eat

you
1. _____
2. _____
3. _____
4. _____

talk

I
1. _____
2. _____
3. _____
4. _____

Skill Objective: Simple present and past, present progressive, future form: *going to*. Have two students pantomime playing baseball. Ask, "What are they doing now?" "What do they do every afternoon?" "What did they do yesterday?" "What are they going to do tomorrow?" Next, write the cue words on the board: *now, every night, last night, tomorrow night*. Have a student pantomime brushing his/her teeth. Let students ask and answer questions, using the cue words. Assign the page for independent work.

Skill Sharpeners 3—Unit 3

Work Places

Read the following paragraphs. Tell where the people work. The first one is done for you.

1. Bill comes to work every day at 7:00. He feeds the animals their breakfast. He makes sure they are feeling well. Right now, he is teaching a monkey to do a new trick.

   Bill works _in a zoo._

2. Susan arrives at work at 8:00. She talks to the news director and the weather forecaster. At 12:00, her program begins. Right now, Susan is reading the news.

   Susan works _____

3. Carlos reports to work at 8:30. He looks at some loan applications. People ask him about loans and different kinds of accounts every day. Right now, Carlos is helping a customer to open a new savings account.

   Carlos works _____

4. Nancy Thomas gets to work at 7:15. Every day she erases the front chalkboard and writes a new exercise for the students to copy. Right now, she is making out a test for her third period class.

   Nancy works _____

5. Dana and Pat work from 9:00 to 5:00. They work together. Every day they answer phones, file papers, and take dictation from the boss. Right now, they are both typing important letters to other companies.

   Dana and Pat work _____

6. Dave begins work at 11:00 P.M. He works until 7:00 in the morning. Every night he stamps prices on cereal, pet food, canned goods, and soda. He arranges food neatly on the shelves. Right now, he is sweeping the floor. Dave wants everything to look good when the boss comes in.

   Dave works _____

7. Alana gets to work at 6:00 A.M. Every day she sits in a tall glass building and watches airplanes take off and land. She talks to the pilots by radio. She tells them when it is their turn to take off. Right now, she is taking a break. Her job is very difficult.

   Alana works _____

8. Lisa works part-time after school. She gets a list from the manager every afternoon. It tells her the rooms she has to clean. Lisa makes the beds and vacuums the rugs. Right now, she is polishing the woodwork in Room 106.

   Lisa works _____

9. Lorraine works from 3:00 P.M. to 11:00 P.M. Every afternoon she checks on her patients. She gives them their medicine and takes their temperature. At night she reads their charts and prepares their medication for the morning. Right now, she is talking with a patient. She is helping him to relax.

   Lorraine works _____

MEMORY BANK

airport   bank   hospital   hotel   office   school   supermarket   TV station   zoo

---

Skill Sharpeners 3—Unit 3

33

Application Forms

If you apply for a part-time job, you will probably be given an application form to fill out. Each company has its own kind of form. But the information you have to give the company is very much the same for all companies. You almost always have to give your name, address, telephone number, and Social Security number. You also have to give the names of the schools you have attended. In addition, companies want to know what other jobs you have had. Finally, they want the names of people who know you and are willing to tell about you. (Before you list such a person as a "reference," be sure to ask his or her permission to do this.)

The sample form on this page gives you a place to write down this kind of information. **Fill it out for yourself. You may want to make a copy to take with you when you apply for a job and have to fill out an application form.**

PERSONAL DATA

Name _____ Social Security Number _____

Address _____ How long at this address _____

_____

Telephone _____

EDUCATION

	Name and Location	Dates Attended (from–to)	Courses
Elementary School			
Junior High or Middle School			
High School			

PREVIOUS JOBS (list latest job first)

From-To	Name and Location of Employer	Supervisor	Position Held and Salary	Reason for Leaving

REFERENCES

		Name and Address	Telephone Number
Personal:	1.		
	2.		
	3.		
Business:	1.		
	2.		
	3.		

*Skill Objective: Filling out an application form
Review this application form with the students, explaining any unfamiliar terms. Discuss possible appropriate responses to: Special Skills, Reason for Leaving Job, and Business References. Assign the page for independent work. Provide individual help as needed.*

Social Security

Social Security is a United States Government program. It pays money to you or your family when you retire, are disabled, are very sick, or die. Social Security is paid for by a "payroll tax." Your employer takes a small part of your pay each pay period. Your employer adds an equal amount from his or her income. This money is sent to the government to help pay for Social Security. Your part is listed on your paycheck or pay slip as FICA (Federal Insurance Contributions Act, the name of the law that set up Social Security).

To get a job, you need a Social Security number. You get a Social Security number by going to the nearest Social Security office and filling out an application form. In a few weeks you will receive a card with your number on it.

You will need to take certain things with you:
- People born in the U.S. need a legal copy of a birth certificate.
- People born outside the U.S. who are now U.S. citizens can bring one of these: (1) a naturalization certificate; (2) a U.S. citizen identity card; (3) a U.S. passport; (4) a certificate of citizenship; (5) a consular report of birth.
- People born outside of the U.S. who are aliens need to bring either an Alien Registration Card (Green Card) or a U.S. Immigration Form.

The form asks you for certain information. Be sure that you know the answers to the following questions. Write the answers here, and make a copy to take with you to the Social Security office.

1. Your full name (the name that you will use in work or business)
   _____

2. The name that was given to you at birth. (This may be the same, or it may not be.)
   _____

3. Your birthplace _____

4. Your date of birth _____

5. Your age at your last birthday _____

6. Your mother's full name at her birth (before she was married) _____
   _____

7. Your father's full name _____

8. Your mailing address (where letters will reach you). Include the zip code.
   _____

9. Your telephone number. (Include the area code.) _____

Skill Sharpeners 3—Unit 3

Let's Go!

Read the story. Then follow the instructions below it.

My friend Carla is always late for school! Every morning at 7:30 I stop by her house because we walk to the bus stop together, and every morning I have to wait five minutes while she finishes breakfast or combs her hair. It really drives me crazy! Her mother says it doesn't make any difference if Carla gets up at six o'clock, six-thirty, or seven, it's just impossible for her to be on time. Some mornings Carla's mother has to drive her to school because she misses the bus. Other mornings Carla and I run to the bus stop while the bus waits for us. All the kids on the bus know who we are. Most of the time I wait for Carla, but there are a few days when her mother tells me to go ahead alone. Sometimes I think I'm crazy to put up with Carla, but she's my good friend and we always go everywhere together.

Now pretend that Carla was a friend of yours a few years ago. Write the story again, but change it from the *present tense* to the *past tense*. Use more paper if you need to. The first sentence is done for you.

My friend Carla was always late for school!

Choose the Verb Form

Present Progressive		Past Progressive
Simple Present	Future (going to)	Simple Past

Use the correct form of the verb in each sentence. Look at the five examples. There is one for each of the five tenses in the box. Use them as a model for your answers.

Examples: (write) 1. Bob _is writing_ a letter now.
          (write) 2. Bob _writes_ a letter to his family every day.
          (write) 3. Bob _wrote_ to his father yesterday.
          (write) 4. Bob _was writing_ to his family when the phone rang.
          (write) 5. Bob _is going to write_ to his family next week.

(play) 1. Every Friday night my brothers _____ cards.

(take) 2. I _____ the bus to school every day.

(do) 3. Susan _____ her homework now.

(take) 4. My class _____ a field trip next week.

(watch) 5. Yesterday Ronald _____ TV for five hours.

(ride) 6. Tomorrow I _____ my bicycle to school.

(drive) 7. At the moment, Mr. and Mrs. Jones _____ to Miami.

(snow) 8. It _____ when I arrived in Chicago.

(have) 9. Marisa _____ a math class at 1:15 every Tuesday.

(read) 10. Mr. Chin _____ a chemistry book when the lights went off.

(see) 11. Last night I _____ a good movie.

(go) 12. Nick _____ to college after he graduates from high school.

(find) 13. Mr. Rodriguez _____ ten dollars in the street yesterday.

(die) 14. Maria's dog _____ three days ago.

(play) 15. Rosita _____ tennis when it started to rain.

(take) 16. Next month Kim _____ a vacation in Tokyo.

(speak) 17. My sister and I _____ five languages.

(sleep) 18. Be quiet! The baby _____.

(cut) 19. Pat _____ her finger while she was slicing tomatoes.

(buy) 20. Henry and John _____ a new car every three years.

Skill Sharpeners 3—Unit 3

I'm Busy, You're Busy

A. Read the story quickly to get a general idea of the subject. Then look at the Vocabulary Highlights. These words are underlined in the story. Be sure you understand the meaning of each word as it is used in the story. Check in the dictionary if you are unsure. Remember, some words have more than one meaning. Write down the meanings of the words that are new to you.

Vocabulary Highlights

internal	destroying
pumps	average
beats	message
breathe	blinking
liquid	growing
filtering	peels

B. Now read the story again. Use the dictionary if there are other words you do not understand.

Busy, Busy, Busy

What machine works night and day without stopping? Your body! Even when you are sleeping, your body is busily working. All of the different systems of your body are in a constant state of activity, 24 hours a day.

Most of this activity is internal, and you are hardly aware of it. For example, your heart pumps about 3,000 gallons of blood each day. It beats about 100,000 times each day. You breathe about 23,000 times a day, putting your lungs to work with every breath you take. Your stomach is busy turning solid food into liquid. Your kidneys are busy cleaning and filtering over 170 quarts of different fluids that run through your body.

All through the day, your body is destroying and replacing cells in the blood. On an average day, the body destroys 250 million red blood cells. That seems like a lot, but you really don't have to worry; you have more than 20 trillion of them in your body.

Your brain is the busiest of all your body parts. No other part of the body functions without first sending a message to the brain. On an average day, the brain receives and acts on more than a million messages from different parts of the body.

Outside of the body, things are happening, too. You are constantly blinking your eyes to keep them clean. Your hair is growing—about two hundredths of an inch every day. Finally, your skin is changing. It peels off very slowly, but by the end of about three weeks, a whole layer of skin is gone. A new layer replaces it. All of this goes on very slowly and quietly; you seldom notice these changes.

Now you know why you are so tired at the end of the day! There's a lot of activity going on inside you even when there doesn't seem to be much going on at all. Make sure to get your rest each night. Your busy body needs it.

(Go on to the next page.)

C. **What is the main idea of this story?**

1. The brain is the busiest part of the human body.
2. The body destroys millions of red blood cells every day.
3. The systems in your body are constantly at work, when you are awake and when you're asleep.
4. To stay healthy, always get a good night's sleep.

D. **Use a word from the Vocabulary Highlights to complete each of these sentences.**

1. The secretary has a _____ for her boss.
2. When ice melts, it turns from solid to _____.
3. Our new cat is too playful; he is _____ our home!
4. The baby is _____ so quickly that she can't fit into her jacket any more.
5. It's hard to look at the sun without _____.

E. **Use the story to answer these questions. Use short answers.**

1. About how many times does your heart beat each day? _____
2. About how many red blood cells does the body destroy each day? _____
3. About how many red blood cells does the average person have? _____
4. About how many messages does the brain receive each day? _____
5. About how much does the average person's hair grow each day? _____

F. **Test your knowledge of body language! Match each action with its corresponding body part by writing the letter of the body part in the blank following the action. Use the dictionary if you need to.**

1. blink or wink _____   a. ankle
2. nod or shake _____   b. tongue
3. sniff or smell _____   c. head
4. lick _____   d. nose
5. grin or whistle _____   e. neck
6. bite _____   f. mouth
7. snap or cross _____   g. eyes
8. crane _____   h. teeth
9. sprain or twist _____   i. fingers
10. stub _____   j. toe

Skill Sharpeners 3—Unit 3

Word Skills: Adding "ing"

When you write verbs in the present continuous and past continuous tenses, you use the ending *ing*. Here are some rules to help you add that ending.

Rule 1: For words that end in a silent (not pronounced) *e*, drop the *e* and add *ing*. Example: *smile, smiling.*

Rule 2: For one-syllable words that end in consonant-vowel-consonant (except *x*), double the last letter and add *ing*. Examples: *sit, sitting; run, running.*

Rule 3: For most other words (including words that end in *y*), add *ing* with no changes. Examples: *rain, raining; send, sending.*

A. Now use these rules to add *ing* to the following words:

1. shave _____
2. comb _____
3. make _____
4. feed _____
5. do _____
6. empty _____
7. jog _____
8. take _____
9. vacuum _____
10. go _____
11. sleep _____
12. wax _____
13. change _____
14. fry _____
15. get _____
16. hope _____
17. jump _____
18. joke _____
19. marry _____
20. put _____
21. say _____
22. talk _____
23. stop _____
24. type _____
25. use _____
26. worry _____
27. look _____
28. bat _____
29. dance _____
30. hurry _____
31. save _____
32. tap _____
33. ferry _____
34. buy _____
35. sew _____
36. eat _____
37. write _____
38. dream _____
39. cut _____
40. roar _____
41. snap _____
42. dig _____
43. bury _____
44. see _____
45. grate _____

B. Now write a sentence on another piece of paper for each of the *ing* words you made. If you wish, you may use more than one *ing* word in a single sentence. For example: *While Dad was _____ing, Bob was _____ing on the telephone and I was upstairs _____ing.*

Dear Dot

Dear Dot—

I am very angry with my children. Six weeks ago they found a puppy and brought it home. They promised me that they were going to feed it and walk it and take care of it. It was so little and cute that I decided they could keep it, even though I don't like dogs very much. Here's my problem: no one takes care of the puppy. I walk it every day. I feed it and clean up after it. No one else can seem to find the time. Dot, I am busy, too, and I don't want to be responsible for this dog. What can I do?

Fido's Nursemaid

1. Who is angry with the children? _____

2. What did the children promise? _____
   _____

3. What does Nursemaid do every day? _____
   _____

4. Why doesn't anyone else take care of the dog? _____
   _____

5. What does the word *promised* in this letter mean? Circle the best answer.

   a. lied   b. broke   c. stole   d. assured

6. What is your advice to Fido's Nursemaid? Discuss your answer in class. Then read Dot's answer and tell why you agree or disagree. Dot's advice is below.

Dear Nursemaid—

Remind your children about their promise to take care of the dog. After supper, keep them at the table until they complete a schedule, showing when each one is going to be responsible for the puppy. If anyone misses a day, give him or her extra chores to do around the house. Tell them that if they don't cooperate, you might have to take the dog to the pound—and remind them about what happens there.

Dot

Write About It

On your paper, make a list of rules or write a paragraph that explains the responsibilities of owning a pet.

Skill Objectives: Reading for details, drawing conclusions, understanding words through context, making judgments. Have students read the letter and answer the questions independently. Students can write their advice to "Fido's Nursemaid" on a separate piece of paper. Correct the first five questions as a class, then have students compare and discuss their own advice and Dot's reply. You may wish to assign the "Write About It" topic as homework.

Skill Sharpeners 3—Unit 3

Paying Bills

To form the present perfect tense, we use *have* or *has* and the past participle of the main verb. Look at these examples with the verb *pay*.

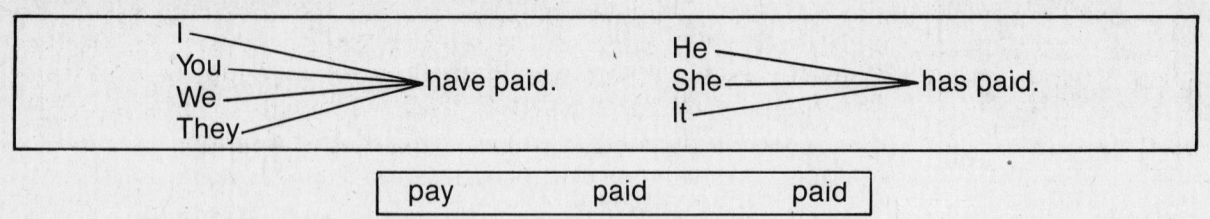

| I / You / We / They | → have paid. | He / She / It | → has paid. |

| pay | paid | paid |

Mr. Rivera has to pay a lot of bills every month. He has to pay the rent, the electric bill, the telephone bill, and so on. On December second he paid the rent. On December fourth he paid the electric bill. On December sixth he paid the oil bill. Today is December eighth. He still has to pay more bills—the gas bill, the doctor, and the telephone. **Look at his bill-paying schedule below and answer the questions.** The first two are done for you.

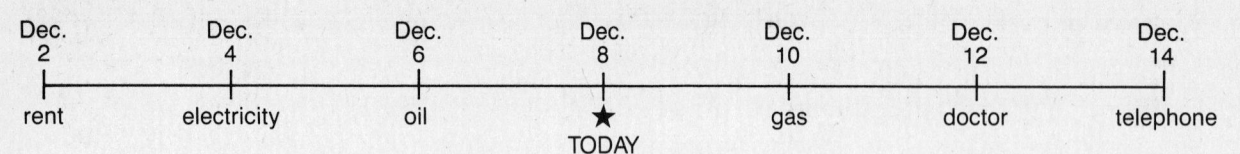

Dec. 2	Dec. 4	Dec. 6	Dec. 8	Dec. 10	Dec. 12	Dec. 14
rent	electricity	oil	★ TODAY	gas	doctor	telephone

1. Has Mr. Rivera paid the rent yet?
   Yes, he has already paid the rent. He paid the rent on December second.

2. Has Mr. Rivera paid the telephone bill yet?
   No he hasn't paid the telephone bill yet. He is going to pay the telephone bill on December fourteenth.

3. Has Mr. Rivera paid the oil bill yet?
   _____
   _____

4. Has Mr. Rivera paid the doctor bill yet?
   _____
   _____

5. Has Mr. Rivera paid the electric bill yet?
   _____
   _____

6. Has Mr. Rivera paid the gas bill yet?
   _____
   _____

Already—Use in affirmative sentences: I have <u>already</u> done my homework.
Already—Means *in the past*: I have <u>already</u> done it. I did it last night.

Yet—Use in questions: Have you done your homework <u>yet</u>?
Yet—Use in negative sentences: I haven't done my homework <u>yet</u>.

Skill Sharpeners 3—Unit 4

The Garcia Family

Every week, Rosita and Jorge Garcia have to help around the house. They have to clean their rooms, walk the dog, empty the trash, iron their clothes, wash the car, and water the plants. **Look at the pictures on this page and use them to answer the questions.** Notice that three of the pictures are under the heading *Yesterday* and three are under the heading *Tomorrow*. The first two questions are done for you. Use them as a model for your answers.

Yesterday   **Today**   **Tomorrow**

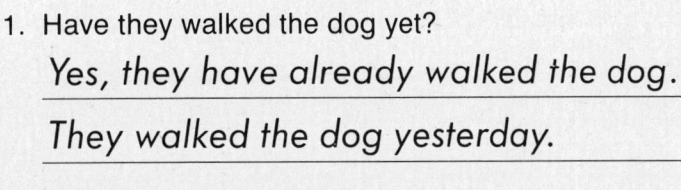

1. Have they walked the dog yet?
   Yes, they have already walked the dog.
   They walked the dog yesterday.

2. Have they washed the car yet?
   No, they haven't washed the car yet, but
   they are going to wash the car tomorrow.

3. Have they watered the plants yet?
   _____
   _____
   _____

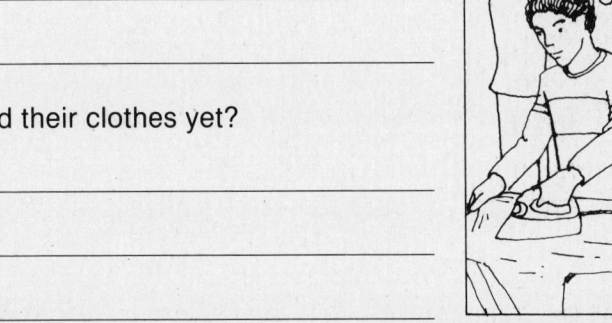

4. Have they ironed their clothes yet?
   _____
   _____
   _____

5. Have they emptied the trash yet?
   _____
   _____
   _____

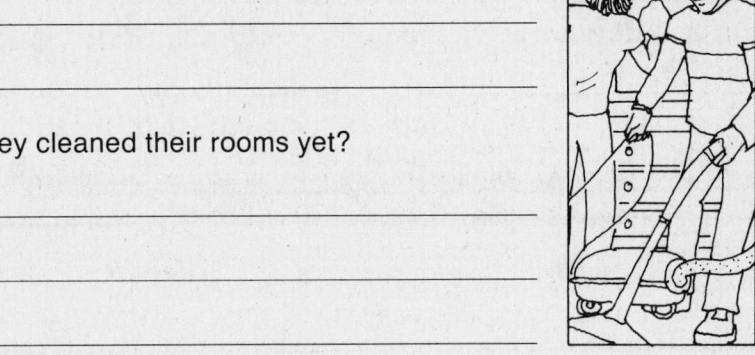

6. Have they cleaned their rooms yet?
   _____
   _____
   _____

Skill Objective: Comparing the present perfect, simple past and future form: *going to*. Go over the directions and sample items with the class. Draw attention to the use and placement of *yet* and *already*. If you wish, provide oral practice by asking students, *Have you finished the page yet? Have you eaten lunch yet? Have you seen the movie . . . yet? Assign the page for independent work.*

Skill Sharpeners 3—Unit 4   43

Carolina's Vacation

Carolina lives in Washington, D.C., and she is going to take a vacation to Walt Disney World in Florida next month. Before she leaves, she has to do many important things. This is Carolina's list of things to do before she goes. She has checked the things she has already completed.

- ✓ call a travel agent
- ✓ make a hotel reservation
- ✓ buy airplane tickets
- ___ mail deposit to hotel
- ✓ shop for some new clothes
- ___ find a comfortable pair of shoes
- ✓ read information about Walt Disney World
- ___ pack suitcase

Use Carolina's checked list to answer the questions. The first two are done for you. Use them as models for your answers.

1. Has Carolina called a travel agent yet?
   Yes, she has already called a travel agent.

2. Has she packed her suitcase yet?
   No, she hasn't packed her suitcase yet.

3. Has she made a hotel reservation yet?

4. Has she bought airplane tickets yet?

5. Has she mailed a deposit to the hotel yet?

6. Has she shopped for some new clothes yet?

7. Has she found a comfortable pair of shoes yet?

8. Has she read information about Disney World yet?

Study and learn these past participles.

buy—bought—*bought*	make—made—*made*
call—called—*called*	pack—packed—*packed*
find—found—*found*	read—read—*read*
mail—mailed—*mailed*	shop—shopped—*shopped*

44 Skill Sharpeners 3—Unit 4

Getting There

This is a map of the Rapid Transit lines of the Massachusetts Bay Transportation Authority (MBTA). The MBTA runs most public transportation in Boston and surrounding cities. Notice that it has four Rapid Transit lines, the Red, Green, Orange, and Blue Lines. **Use the map to answer the questions under it. Use more paper if you need to; be sure your answers are complete.** The first one is done for you.

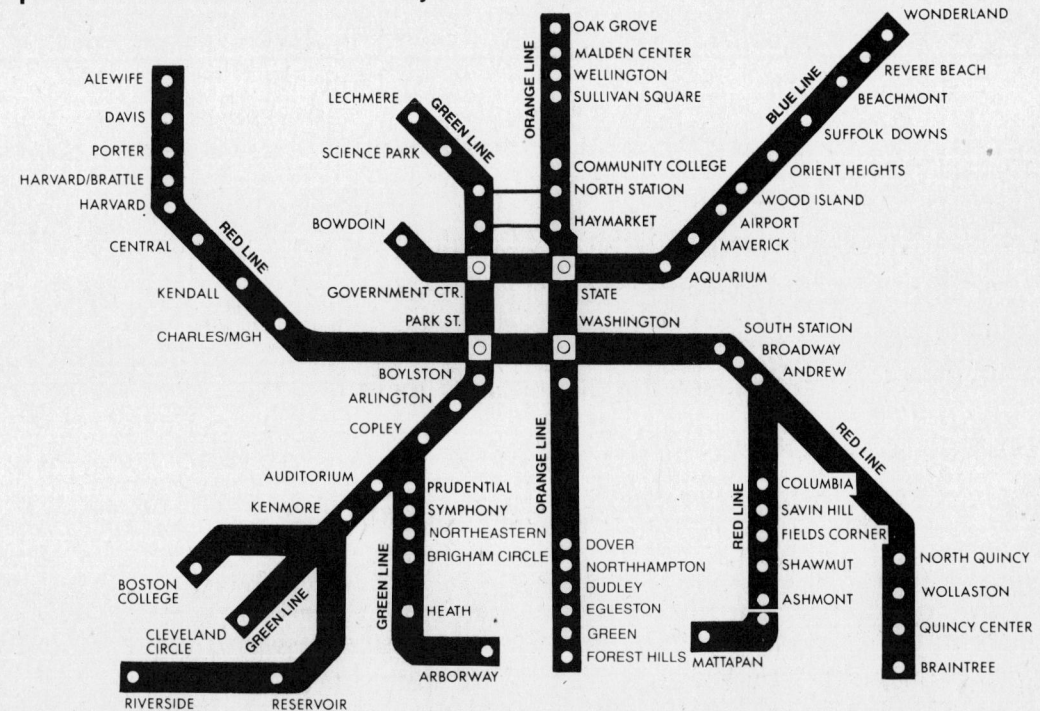

1. Using the MBTA, how can you get from North Quincy to Haymarket?
   Take the Red Line north and get off at Washington. Get on to an Orange Line train going north and ride to Haymarket, which is the second stop.

2. You're at Harvard and want to go to Aquarium. How do you go?

3. How can you get from Forest Hills to Sullivan Square?

4. How can you get from Orient Heights to Copley?

5. How can you get from Boston College to Community College?

6. You get on a train at Ashmont (going north) and get off at Park Street. You get on an Arborway train on the Green Line (going south) and get off at the fifth stop. Where are you?

7. You park your car at Wonderland and take the MBTA to Government Center. Then you take the Green Line north for three stops. Where are you?

Skill Sharpeners 3—Unit 4

The Declaration of Independence

A. Read the story quickly to get a general idea of the subject. Then look at the Vocabulary Highlights. These words are underlined in the story. Be sure you understand the meaning of each word as it is used in the story. Check in the dictionary if you are unsure. Remember, some words have more than one meaning. Write down the meanings of the words that are new to you.

Vocabulary Highlights

document	simplified
created	accusations
equal	forced
preventing	protected
interfering	refused

B. Now read the story again. Use the dictionary if there are other words you do not understand.

An Important Document

The Declaration of Independence is an important document in the history of the United States. Thomas Jefferson is the author of this great work. He wrote it long before he was President of the United States. The first part of the Declaration of Independence says that all men are created equal and that they have a right to life, liberty, and happiness. In the second part of the Declaration, Jefferson explained that the King of England was preventing the colonists from having these rights.

To show the world exactly how the King was interfering with the freedoms of the colonists, Thomas Jefferson included in the Declaration of Independence a long list of the King's policies in the colonies. Here is a shortened and simplified list of the accusations Thomas Jefferson made against the King of England:

1. He has taxed us against our wishes.
2. He has deprived us of our rights.
3. He has ordered British soldiers into our homes.
4. He has burned our towns.
5. He has forced Americans to serve in the British navy.
6. He has helped the Indians to attack western villages.
7. He has protected British soldiers who have murdered innocent colonists.
8. He has closed down some of our Houses of Representatives.
9. He has refused to let us have elections.
10. He has passed laws that have hurt the American people.

Thomas Jefferson ended the Declaration of Independence by saying that the thirteen colonies were no longer part of the British Empire. They did not belong to the King any more. The colonies were now the United States of America. They were a new nation in a new world.

(Go on to the next page.)

C. Often you can *draw a conclusion* from something you read. That is, you can figure out the answer to a question even though that answer is not stated in the reading. **Draw a conclusion to complete the following sentence. Circle your answer.**

The colonists wanted to be independent because

a. all men are created equal.
b. the King treated them unfairly.
c. they wanted to be the United States of America.
d. all men have a right to liberty and happiness.

D. **Use a word from the Vocabulary Highlights to complete each of these sentences.**

1. The work was too hard for the students, so the teacher _____ it.

2. The waiter cut the cake in six _____ pieces.

3. The striking workers shouted _____ in front of the factory.

4. I asked my boss for a raise but he _____ to give it to me.

5. Many politicians signed their names to this _____.

E. **Use separate paper to write answers to these questions.**

1. Who is the author of the Declaration of Independence?
2. What rights do all Americans have, according to the Declaration?
3. Who was keeping these rights from the colonists?
4. How did Thomas Jefferson end the Declaration of Independence?
5. What was the new name for the American colonies?

F. **Find details in the story that best complete the following outline.**

THE DECLARATION OF INDEPENDENCE

A. The Introduction (The First Part)
　1. _____
　2. _____
B. The Accusations Against the King
　1. _____
　2. _____
　3. _____
　4. _____
　5. _____
C. The Conclusion (The Ending)
　1. _____
　2. _____

Skill Sharpeners 3—Unit 4

Word Skills: Adding "ed"

When you write the past tense and the past participle of regular verbs, you use the ending *ed*. Here are some rules to help you add that ending.

Rule 1: For words that already end in *e*, simply add the letter *d*. Examples: *love, loved; like, liked.*

Rule 2: For words that end in a consonant followed by *y*, change the *y* to *i* and add *ed*. Examples: *marry, married; hurry, hurried.*

Rule 3: For most words that end in a vowel followed by *y*, simply add *ed* with no changes. Examples: *play, played; stay, stayed.*

Rule 4: For one-syllable words that end in consonant-vowel-consonant (except *x*), double the last letter and add *ed*. (NOTE: Never double final *x*.) Examples: *stop, stopped; jog, jogged.*

Rule 5: For most other words (including words that end in *x*), simply add *ed* with no changes. Examples: *wish, wished; enter, entered.*

A. Now use these rules to add *ed* to the following words:

1. study _____
2. destroy _____
3. clean _____
4. empty _____
5. walk _____
6. scrub _____
7. call _____
8. change _____
9. close _____
10. shop _____
11. hate _____
12. listen _____
13. plant _____
14. shave _____
15. worry _____
16. dance _____
17. brush _____
18. drop _____
19. pray _____
20. crash _____
21. wait _____
22. wash _____
23. bake _____
24. ask _____
25. carry _____
26. copy _____
27. cry _____
28. deliver _____
29. dress _____
30. fry _____
31. obey _____
32. bury _____
33. type _____
34. hum _____
35. open _____
36. fill _____
37. dirty _____
38. laugh _____
39. roast _____
40. dry _____
41. enjoy _____
42. answer _____
43. name _____
44. trot _____
45. fix _____

B. Now write a sentence on another piece of paper for each of the *ed* words you made. If you wish, you may use more than one *ed* word in a single sentence. For example: *Before she _____ed, she _____ed her clothes.*

48

Skill Sharpeners 3—Unit 4

Dear Dot

Dear Dot—

My father is a grouch. When he comes home, he never says "hello" or asks how I am. Instead he says, "Have you done your homework?" or "Have you cleaned your room?" His other favorite question is "Have you emptied the trash?" His first question to my mother is, "Have you cooked dinner yet?" After dinner he isn't quite as grouchy, but he's never in a really good mood. I can't stand much more of his grouchiness. I have thought of getting my own apartment, but I am only sixteen and still in school. What can I do?

Donna

1. What questions does Donna's father ask her when he comes home? _____

2. What question does he ask her mother? _____

3. When is Donna's father less grouchy? _____

4. What has Donna thought of doing? _____

5. What does the word *mood* in this letter mean? Circle the best answer.

   a. room   b. state of mind   c. verb   d. change of heart

6. What is your advice to Donna? Discuss your answer in class. Then read Dot's answer and tell why you agree or disagree. Dot's advice is below.

Dear Donna—

Do your homework. Clean your room. Empty the trash. There really isn't a way to cheer your father up. Some people are just not happy people, but you can do your best to avoid fights and arguments by doing what he wants as much as possible. It seems difficult now, but someday you will have your own apartment—and you might even miss the "old grouch."

Dot

Write About It

On your paper, write a descriptive paragraph about a happy person. Tell what he or she looks like and what the person's attitude toward life is. (You may be the subject of your own paragraph if you think you are that kind of person.)

Skill Sharpeners 3—Unit 4

Can You? Could You?

A. Answer these questions. The first two are done for you. Use them as models.

1. Can you speak English? __Yes, I can.__
2. Could you speak English last summer? __No, I couldn't.__
3. Can you ride a horse? _____
4. Could you find your shoes this morning? _____
5. Can you type? _____
6. Could you tell time when you were four years old? _____

B. Complete the sentence with *can, can't, could,* or *couldn't*. The first one is done for you.

1. Today, in many cities, girls __can__ take an auto mechanics course in high school. Twenty years ago, girls _____ take this course in most schools.
2. If you are not an American citizen, you _____ vote for President.
3. A good runner, like Margarita, _____ run more than five miles in half an hour.
4. As a boy, Mr. Ruiz was a good football player. He _____ play very well.
5. Pam and Sam _____ go to the beach yesterday because it was raining hard.
6. Emily Yee lives in San Francisco. On sunny days, she _____ see the Golden Gate Bridge from her window, but on foggy days she _____.
7. If you use the yellow pages, you _____ find the number of a hospital.
8. Because Beethoven was deaf, he _____ hear the last symphonies he wrote.
9. There was lots of snow last winter, so Kevin _____ go skiing often.
10. Twenty years ago in most high schools, boys _____ take a cooking course, but now they _____ take one.
11. I like to listen to music, but I _____ play the piano at all.
12. Carmen is blind now, but when she was young, she _____ see very well.

Skill Sharpeners 3—Unit 5

Do You Have To?

A. Complete the following sentences by using *have to*, *has to* or *had to*.
The first one is done for you.

1. Carla ____has to____ study tonight.

2. My parents _____ pay a lot of bills every month.

3. You _____ take Physics I before you can take Physics II.

4. Lisa couldn't attend the meeting because she _____ visit her mother in the hospital.

5. My mother said I _____ vacuum the living room before I could go to the ball game.

6. My grandfather _____ weed his garden every week.

7. Mr. and Mrs. Ruiz _____ move to a different apartment after the fire destroyed their building.

8. Does Vuong _____ walk the dog when he gets home?

9. John's grandfather _____ wear his glasses when he reads the newspaper.

10. Did you _____ call the doctor about your problem?

11. You _____ insure the package before you mail it.

12. I _____ go to the doctor for a checkup yesterday.

B. Excuses, Excuses! Think of three good excuses for each of the following situations. Use *had to* or *have to*. The first one is done for you. Use it as a model.

Why didn't you do your homework?
1. *I had to cook dinner for my family.*
2. _____
3. _____

Why can't you help me with the housework?
1. _____
2. _____
3. _____

Why couldn't Carla come to my party?
1. She _____
2. _____
3. _____

Skill Objective: Using *have to*, *has to*, *had to*. Ask several students questions. Write their responses on the board. What do you have to do after school today? What did you have to do last weekend? Then ask their classmates: What does (Ana) have to do today? What do (Ravi and Lars) have to do? What did . . . have to do last week? Assign Part A for independent work. Students may work on Part B in pairs. Encourage students to share their excuses with their classmates.

Skill Sharpeners 3—Unit 5

Have You Ever?

A. Interview three of your classmates to get answers for the ten questions below. Make notes of each student's responses on the chart.

	(Name)	(Name)	(Name)
1. Have you ever eaten dinner at midnight? When?			
2. Have you ever met a famous person? Who?			
3. Have you ever found money in the street? How much?			
4. Have you ever cooked dinner for your family? What?			
5. Have you ever been to Walt Disney World? When?			
6. Have you ever slept until noon? How often?			
7. Have you ever had a job? What?			
8. Have you ever been in the hospital? When? Why?			
9. Have you ever traveled by plane? Where?			
10. Have you ever tried Italian food? What?			

B. Use the results of your interviews to write a paragraph about your classmates. Use more paper if you need to. The first sentence is done for you.

My classmates have done many interesting things.

_____
_____
_____
_____
_____
_____

Skill Objectives: Using present perfect, interviewing, writing an informative paragraph

Have a student interview first you, then several classmates with the first few questions. Model the correct answer structures. Show how to note the essential information on the interview chart. Point out the use of simple past vs. present perfect. Note that the second question is asked only if the first answer is yes. Provide as much group practice as needed, then have students form pairs and interview each other.

Skill Sharpeners 3—Unit 5

Have You Seen *Star Wars*?

A. Kim and Lee like to go to the movies. Sometimes they see the same movie again and again. Here are some movies Kim and Lee have seen. **Use this list to answer the questions below it.** The first two questions are answered for you. Use them as a model.

May, 1978: *Rocky*	May, 1979: *Dracula*	July, 1981: *Star Wars*
June, 1978: *Star Wars*	April, 1980: *Star Wars*	March, 1982: *Rocky*
January, 1979: *Rocky*	February, 1981: *Dracula*	

1. How many times have Kim and Lee seen *Star Wars*? *They have seen Star Wars three times.*

2. When did Kim and Lee first see *Star Wars*? *They first saw Star Wars in June, 1978.*

3. How many times have they seen *Rocky*? _____

4. When did they first see *Rocky*? _____

5. How many times have they seen *Dracula*? _____

6. When did they first see *Dracula*? _____

B. Carlotta likes to travel. Here are some of the places to which she has traveled. **Use this list to answer the questions.**

January, 1981: Paris	November, 1981: Paris	August, 1982: Rome
May, 1981: Rome	February, 1982: Paris	March, 1983: Madrid

1. How many times has Carlotta been to Paris? _____
2. When did she first go there? _____
3. Has she ever been to Rome? _____
4. How many times has she been there? _____
5. Has she ever been to Madrid? _____
6. How many times has she been there? _____

MEMORY BANK

see/saw/<u>seen</u>   am-is-are/was-were/<u>been</u>

Skill Sharpeners 3—Unit 5

A True Genius

A. Read the story quickly to get a general idea of the subject. Then look at the Vocabulary Highlights. These words are underlined in the story. Be sure you understand the meaning of each word as it is used in the story. Check in the dictionary if you are unsure. Remember, some words have more than one meaning. Write down the meanings of the words that are new to you.

Vocabulary Highlights

perfected	sockets
public	supply
laboratory	substitute
dynamos	shortage
wires, wiring	genius

B. Now read the story again. Use the dictionary if there are other words you do not understand.

Thomas Edison

Most people know that Thomas Edison invented the first working light bulb, but they don't know anything else about him. Edison had almost no formal schooling, he had a hearing loss most of his life, yet he invented over 1,000 different things. Among Edison's most successful inventions are: the electric vote recorder, the phonograph (record player), the dictating machine, the mimeograph (duplicator), the movie camera, and the movie projector.

Thomas Edison perfected his electric light bulb in 1879, but there was still much work to do before his invention was useful to the public. Only scientists used electricity at that time. No one knew how to use electricity safely outside of a laboratory before Thomas Edison. He and his workers had to create a safe and workable electric system.

Edison and his workers had a big job to do. First they had to build a factory. Then they had to build the dynamos (generators) to make the electricity. Next they had to put up wires to send out the electricity, and finally they had to install electric wiring and sockets in people's houses so that they could use the electricity.

Thomas Edison wanted to light up the United States electrically. To show people that he was serious, Edison began his project in New York City. It was America's largest city at that time. If Edison could bring electricity to New York, he could bring it anywhere.

By 1887, much of New York City had electricity. Edison formed the Edison Electric Light Company and continued to supply electricity to New York City and other places. His new factory, in West Orange, New Jersey, made the machines and equipment.

Thomas Edison lived until 1931. He continued to invent and perfect inventions all his life. He worked for the United States Navy in World War I. After the war, he tried to invent a substitute for rubber because of the shortage that the war caused.

Thomas Edison was a true genius, but he never went to a college or university. He was completely self-taught. The only time Edison attended school was when he was seven years old. He stayed for three months and never returned. Thomas Edison was a school dropout, yet he became one of America's most famous and most honored men.

(Go on to the next page.)

C. Draw a conclusion from the story to complete the following sentence. Circle your answer.

To make money with his invention, Edison realized that he had to

a. bring electricity to the homes of the United States.
b. invent the light bulb.
c. invent the phonograph.
d. study at a university.

D. Use a word from the Vocabulary Highlights to complete each of these sentences.

1. Margarine is a _____ for butter.

2. Several scientists work in that _____.

3. We don't have any more paper; there is a _____ in the school.

4. James worked for five years before he _____ his invention.

5. Tommy can solve any problem; he's a _____.

E. Use separate paper to write answers to these questions.

1. How many different things did Thomas Edison invent?
2. What are some of Edison's major inventions?
3. What did Edison have to do after he perfected the light bulb?
4. Where did Edison start the first electric system? Why there?
5. What did Edison call his company?
6. What did Edison do during World War I?
7. Why did he try to invent a substitute for rubber?
8. How did Thomas Edison learn so much about science?
9. When did he attend school?
10. How long did he stay in school?

F. Match the beginnings of the sentences at the left with their endings at the right. Write the letter of the correct ending in the blank after the beginning.

1. Students had to read by candle, gas, or oil _____
2. Astronomers had to study the stars with the naked eye _____
3. Secretaries had to write notes and letters by hand _____
4. Cowboys had to reload their guns after every shot _____
5. Prospectors had to blast open mines with gunpowder _____
6. People had to walk up stairs in all buildings _____
7. People had to fasten their clothing with buttons and pins _____

a. until Whitcomb Judson invented the zipper.
b. until Alfred Nobel invented dynamite.
c. until Elisha Otis invented the elevator.
d. until Samuel Colt invented the six-shooter pistol.
e. until Johannes Kepler invented the astronomical telescope.
f. until Thomas Edison invented the light bulb.
g. until Christopher Sholes invented the typewriter.

Skill Sharpeners 3—Unit 5

Word Skills: Synonyms

Words that have the same or nearly the same meaning are called synonyms. *Leave* and *depart* are synonyms because they mean the same thing: The bus *leaves* at 3:00; the bus *departs* at 3:00. **Read each sentence. Find a synonym for the underlined word in the Memory Bank at the bottom of the page and write it on the line following the sentence.** The first one is done for you.

1. The car isn't working; Felix is trying to fix it.   *repair*
2. Lorenzo's books are downstairs in the basement. _____
3. The scouts are going camping in the forest this weekend. _____
4. The houses on this road are beautiful. _____
5. Class is going to start in ten minutes. _____
6. The library is going to show a French movie this afternoon. _____
7. This shirt was very cheap; I got it on sale. _____
8. The teacher told the children not to act silly. _____
9. Bob exercises every day; he feels great. _____
10. My friend hasn't answered my letter; I'm nervous about that. _____
11. Larry was sad when his vacation was over. _____
12. Lucio is emptying the trash this week. _____
13. Please close the door when you leave. _____
14. Please don't talk to me when I am driving. _____
15. The boys have to hurry because they are late. _____
16. Mr. Chin was angry about losing his watch. _____
17. Tom's home is a very comfortable place to be. _____
18. Everyone in the club was happy to meet Professor Klein. _____
19. Chipmunks and mice are little animals. _____
20. New York and Los Angeles are big cities. _____

MEMORY BANK

begin	cellar	film	foolish	garbage	glad	house
inexpensive	large	mad	repair	rush	shut	small
speak	street	unhappy	wonderful	woods	worried	

56   Skill Sharpeners 3—Unit 5

Dear Dot

Dear Dot—

We are going to have to move soon, and my husband and I are having trouble deciding where to go. I want to stay in the city. Fred wants to buy a house way out in the suburbs. He works at home, so he isn't going to have to commute. But I am going to have to drive 35 miles to work every day. I am going to have to get up earlier, and arrive home later each evening. Besides, I love the city and I hate to drive! Dot, we don't know what to do. How can we compromise?

City Lover

1. What are City Lover and her husband going to have to do soon? _____

2. What does her husband want to do? _____

3. Why does City Lover not want to do what her husband wants? _____

4. What does the word *commute* in this letter mean? Circle your answer.
   a. speak with someone   b. add up   c. arrange something   d. drive to and from a place

5. What is your advice to City Lover? Discuss your answer in class. Then read Dot's answer and tell why you agree or disagree. Dot's advice is below.

Dear City Lover—

Find a closer suburb, if you can. Unfortunately, there may be no easy solution to your problem. One person is probably going to have to give up more than the other. Try to reward the person who gives up the most in other ways. If you move to another place in the city, try to find a quiet, pleasant area and be sure to plan for lots of country weekends. If you have to commute from the country, then perhaps your husband should take over more of the housework. He can also meet you for evenings in the city.

Dot

Write About It

Where would you like to live? On your paper, write a paragraph about the advantages of living in the area of your choice (city, country, or suburbs).

Skill Sharpeners 3—Unit 5

Skill Objectives: Reading for details, understanding words through context, making judgments, supporting an opinion in writing

Have students read the letter and answer the questions independently. Students can write their advice to "City Lover" on a separate piece of paper. Correct the first four questions as a class, then have students compare and discuss their own advice and Dot's reply. You may wish to assign the "Write About It" topic as homework.

The Party

A. As you read the story to yourself, change the verbs in parentheses to the past tense. Then write the whole story with the past tense verbs. Use more paper if you need to.

I am so embarrassed! Here's my story. Last week my girlfriend Astrid (invite) me to a party at her house. She (tell) me that all our friends (are) coming, and also the new boy who just (move) in across the street. I (am) excited about the party, and I (want) to make a good impression. I (go) to Lord and Taylor and (buy) a new pair of slacks and a beautiful new blouse. I also (find) a nice pair of shoes. I (decide) to go to the hairdresser, too. I (spend) a lot of money. When I (get) home from the hairdresser's, I (take) a bath and (put) on my new clothes. I (think) I (look) great! I (feel) happy and excited about the party.

At eight-thirty, I (walk) over to Astrid's house and (ring) the doorbell. Astrid (answer) and (say), "Oh, hi, Luisa. What are you doing here?" I (say) "The party's tonight, isn't it?" She (say), "Oh, no! The party isn't tonight, it's tomorrow night!"

I (feel) so stupid. I (go) to the party on the wrong night!

B. Now read each of the sentences below. Circle T if the sentence is true. Circle F if it is false.

T F 1. Astrid is the person who was giving the party.
T F 2. Luisa is the person who went to the party on the wrong night.
T F 3. Luisa wanted to impress the new neighbor across the street.
T F 4. Luisa bought a new dress for the party.
T F 5. When Luisa got home from the store, she took a shower.
T F 6. Luisa was happy with the way she looked.
T F 7. When Astrid answered the door, she probably looked puzzled.
T F 8. Luisa was embarrassed because she was too late for the party.
T F 9. Luisa probably forgot to ask when the party was.

C. On your paper, write about an embarrassing experience you have had. Tell what happened, when and where it happened, and how you felt about it.

A Nation of Immigrants (1)

A. Look at the two graphs on this page. They show the number of people who immigrated (came into) the United States in each ten-year period from 1821 to 1980. They also show where these people came from. Use the graphs to complete the sentences. The first one is done for you.

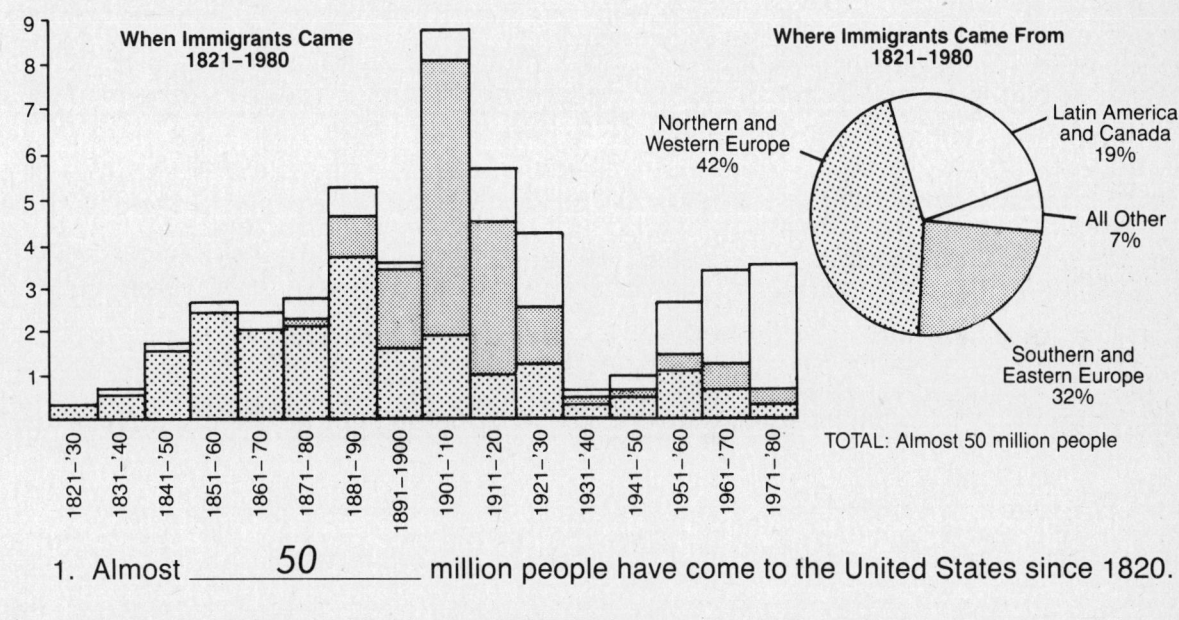

When Immigrants Came 1821–1980 (bar graph, millions, by decade 1821–'30 through 1971–'80)

Where Immigrants Came From 1821–1980 (pie chart)
- Northern and Western Europe 42%
- Latin America and Canada 19%
- All Other 7%
- Southern and Eastern Europe 32%

TOTAL: Almost 50 million people

1. Almost ____50____ million people have come to the United States since 1820.

2. Most of the people who first came were from _____.

3. Most of the people who come now are from _____.

4. People from Southern and Eastern Europe were the largest number of immigrants in the period from _____ to _____.

5. About _____ million people came from Northern and Western Europe between 1821 and 1980.

6. About _____ million immigrants came to the United States between 1901 and 1910.

7. About _____ million immigrants have come from Latin America and Canada since 1821.

8. People from _____ started coming around 1870.

9. Not many immigrants came between 1930 and 1940 probably because _____ _____ (Hint: look at page 12.)

10. The round graph is called a "pie chart" because _____ _____

B. The United States has been called "a nation of immigrants." On your paper, write a paragraph telling why this is or is not a good name. Are there any people in the United States who are not immigrants or descendants of immigrants? Discuss your answer with others in the class.

Skill Objectives: Interpreting graphs, writing a paragraph
Read the introductory paragraph, then draw attention to the pie graph. Ask, Where have most U.S. immigrants come from? Where did your family come from? How many U.S. immigrants have come from that part of the world? Examine the bar graph. Note the shading for the immigrants' homeland is the same in both graphs. Ask, How many immigrants came from... between (1911 and 1920)? Between (1861 and 1870), where did most immigrants come from? Assign the page for independent work.

Skill Sharpeners 3—Unit 6   59

A Nation of Immigrants (2)

On the preceding page are graphs showing the history of immigration into the United States. On this page are tables dealing with immigration for the nine-year period, 1971 to 1979. **Look at these tables. Then do Parts A and B below.**

Table 1. Where Immigrants Came From

Place	Number	Place	Number
Mexico	550,000	Vietnam	130,000
Philippines	310,000	Dominican Rep.	125,000
Cuba	260,000	Italy	120,000
Korea	220,000	Great Britain	118,000
West Indies*	210,000	Portugal	95,000
India	150,000	Greece	90,000
Canada	140,000	Haiti	60,000

*Without Cuba, Dominican Republic, Haiti

Table 2. Percents by Region

Region	Percent
Latin America	48.9%
Asia	16.7%
Europe	16.5%
Canada	5.6%
Other	12.3%

A. Answer these questions. Use the encyclopedia if you need to. The first one is started for you.

1. What are three countries on Table 1 in which the people speak Spanish? _Mexico,_ _____

2. What are two countries on Table 1 in which the people speak English? _____

3. What are three European countries on the table? _____

4. What are three Asian countries on the table? _____

B. Read each of the following statements. Use the tables and your answers on Part A to decide whether it is true or false. Circle T if it is true. Circle F if it is false. The first one is done for you.

(T) F 1. Most of the people who came to the United States between 1971 and 1979 spoke Spanish.

T F 2. Between 1971 and 1979, the number of Cubans who came was double the number of Vietnamese.

T F 3. More people came from Italy than from Korea.

T F 4. The second largest group to come during this period was from Great Britain.

T F 5. More people came from Asia, Europe, and Canada than from Latin America.

T F 6. "Other" includes, Cuba, Dominican Republic, and Haiti.

T F 7. Almost the same percentage of Europeans came as did Canadians.

C. On your paper, make graphs of the information on Tables 1 and 2.

60 Skill Sharpeners 3—Unit 6

Persons and Places

A. Read each sentence. Use the Memory Bank to find the person it describes. The first one is done for you.

1. He's a person who helps you plan a vacation or trip. _travel agent_
2. She's a person who writes books, plays, or stories. _____
3. He's a person who cuts meat at the supermarket. _____
4. She's a person who fills cavities and pulls teeth. _____
5. He's a person who stays with young children when their parents go out for the evening. _____
6. She's a person who gives you information when you dial 411 or 1-555-1212. _____
7. He's a person who decides if a baseball player is out or is safe. _____
8. She's a person who leads a chorus or an orchestra. _____

B. Use the Memory Bank to find the place each sentence describes. The first one is done for you.

1. It's a place where there is lots of sand and very little rain. _desert_
2. It's a place where people play basketball. _____
3. It's a place where you go to wash your clothes. _____
4. It's a place where you go when you want to shop in many different kinds of stores. _____
5. It's a place where you go to see clowns, animals, and acrobats. _____
6. It's a place where you go to see famous paintings and drawings. _____
7. It's a place where you go to buy a watch or a necklace. _____
8. It's a place where you go to buy a sofa or a bed. _____

MEMORY BANK

author	babysitter	butcher	circus	conductor	court
dentist	desert	furniture store	jewelry store	laundromat	mall
museum	operator	travel agent	umpire		

C. Finish these sentences. Use who or where in each sentence. The first one is done for you.

1. An astronaut _is a person who travels in space._
2. A lawyer _____
3. A stadium _____
4. A zoo _____
5. An architect _____

Skill Sharpeners 3—Unit 6

What Did You See?

A. Read the pairs of sentences. Make each pair of sentences into one sentence. Look at the example, and use it as a model for your answers.

Example: Yesterday I saw a man. He was sleeping in the subway station.

Yesterday I saw a man who was sleeping in the subway station.

1. Yesterday I saw a girl. She was walking six dogs at one time!

2. Yesterday I saw an old woman. She was looking in trash cans for food.

3. Yesterday I saw a man. He was wearing a clown costume and handing out papers about the circus.

4. Yesterday I saw a boy. He was roller skating down a busy street.

5. Yesterday I saw a girl. She was eating three ice cream cones at the same time.

6. Yesterday I saw a young man on the subway. He was taking a box of kittens to the pet store.

B. Now use the pictures to write the third line of the dialogue. The first one is done for you.

1. —Do you know Rita Marini?
   —No, I don't. Who is she?
   She's the girl who lives next door to me.

2. —Do you know Kinchee Chow?
   —No, I don't. Who is she?

Skill Sharpeners 3—Unit 6

Word Skills: Prefixes

A prefix is a syllable or group of syllables that comes at the beginning of a word and has a special meaning. You can add a prefix to another word or root word to change the meaning of the original word or to create a new word. **Look at the list of common prefixes below and the examples of each one.**

Prefix and Meaning

Prefix	Meaning	Example	Definition
mono	= one	monorail	train running on one rail
bi	= two	bicycle	two-wheeled vehicle
tri	= three	triangle	three-sided figure
poly	= many	polytheism	belief in many gods
un	= not	unwelcome	not welcome or wanted
pre	= before	prehistoric	before recorded history
ex	= out	export	send out of a country
sub	= under	subterranean	under the ground
inter	= between	international	between nations
re	= again	reread	read again

Now match the columns. Write the letter of the correct definition in the space next to the word. Use your dictionary if you need to. The first one is done for you.

_b_ 1. premature
___ 2. monotone
___ 3. bilingual
___ 4. exhale
___ 5. subtitle
___ 6. interstellar
___ 7. polygon
___ 8. tripod
___ 9. unprepared
___ 10. reorder
___ 11. preface
___ 12. monopoly
___ 13. extract
___ 14. biweekly
___ 15. subway
___ 16. triple
___ 17. polygamy
___ 18. interfere
___ 19. rewrite
___ 20. uncertain

a. speaks two languages
b. before the expected time
c. copy or write again
d. one company in control of an entire business
e. to remove or pull out
f. not ready
g. multiply by three
h. many-sided figure
i. translation on a foreign film
j. one constant tone of voice
k. come between
l. not sure
m. train that travels under the ground
n. breathe out
o. between the stars
p. ask for supplies again
q. every two weeks
r. three-legged support
s. introduction to a book, foreword
t. many wives for one husband

Skill Sharpeners 3—Unit 6

The Iron Horse

A. Read the story quickly to get a general idea of the subject. Then look at the Vocabulary Highlights. These words are underlined in the story. Be sure you understand the meaning of each word as it is used in the story. Check in the dictionary if you are unsure. Remember, some words have more than one meaning. Write down the meanings of the words that are new to you.

Vocabulary Highlights

steam	bet
coal	publicity
iron	accept
owned	catch up
race	extended

B. Now read the story again. Use the dictionary if there are other words you do not understand.

The First Railroads

In the early days of the railroads, horses pulled the trains. The trains had no engines and no power of their own. Richard Trevithik of England invented a <u>steam</u>-powered engine in 1804. He used the engine to pull open cars full of <u>coal</u>. Soon people were building railroads and steam engines all over the world. Because the steam engines did the work that animals used to do, people called them <u>iron</u> horses.

Peter Cooper was a rich American businessman. He <u>owned</u> a lot of land near one of the new American railroads, the Baltimore and Ohio Railroad. He wanted the B&O railroad to be successful. He built his own steam engine to drive along the railroad. The train that Cooper built was very small. It was almost like a toy. Cooper called the train Tom Thumb after the storybook character who was only as big as a thumb.

Most people traveled in stagecoaches drawn by horses. A stagecoach line challenged Peter Cooper to a <u>race</u>. The owner of the line <u>bet</u> his horse could go faster than the train. Cooper agreed to the race. He wanted to get <u>publicity</u> for the new steam engine. He wanted people to <u>accept</u> the railroad.

The day of the race came. At first the horse was winning the race. The horse was able to begin the race at top speed. Tom Thumb needed time to build up steam. Peter Cooper worked hard to make the train go faster. Soon he was <u>catching up</u> to the horse. Finally, he caught up to the horse. After a while he went in front of the horse. Tom Thumb and Peter Cooper were going to win the race! Suddenly one of the parts of the engine broke. The train stopped. The horse rushed ahead. Peter Cooper and Tom Thumb lost the race.

Of course, that is not the end of the story. Other inventors built large and fast trains to replace Tom Thumb. Soon horses couldn't compete with the new trains. By 1870, railroads <u>extended</u> all across the United States. The "iron horse" had become an important part of American life.

(Go on to the next page.)

Skill Sharpeners 3—Unit 6

C. Use a word or phrase from the Vocabulary Highlights to complete each of these sentences.

1. Advertising is a form of _____.

2. The gambler _____ all his money on one card game.

3. My brother left ten minutes ago; I hope I can _____ with him.

4. Some _____ is burned to make electricity.

5. A marathon is a 26-mile _____.

D. Use separate paper to write answers to these questions.

1. In what year did Richard Trevithik invent the railroad steam engine?
2. What did people call the new trains?
3. Why did they use this name?
4. What did Peter Cooper want?
5. What did *Tom Thumb* look like?
6. What was *Tom Thumb* racing against?
7. Why didn't *Tom Thumb* go fast right away?
8. Why did Peter Cooper lose the race?
9. What replaced *Tom Thumb*?
10. By 1870, how far did railroads extend?

E. Americans have always made up names for widely used inventions. Some of these names are in the column at the left. See if you can match them up with the inventions they name. **Write the letter for the invention in the blank in front of the "folk" name for it.**

_____ 1. talking machine   a. television
_____ 2. flying machine   b. aircraft carrier
_____ 3. talkies   c. electric voice amplifier
_____ 4. tin lizzie   d. coin operated phonograph
_____ 5. boob tube   e. record player
_____ 6. nickelodeon   f. tall building
_____ 7. bullhorn   g. movies with sound
_____ 8. skyscraper   h. helicopter
_____ 9. flattop   i. Ford car
_____ 10. whirlybird   j. airplane

F. Imagine it is 1804. People are arguing about whether trains have a future, or if America should stick with horses. **Write three arguments for each side.**

Advantages of a Horse	Advantages of Trains
1.	1.
2.	2.
3.	3.

Skill Sharpeners 3—Unit 6

Dear Dot

Dear Dot—

My friend Larry asked me to lend him one of my records last week. I am very careful with my records, and I don't usually let people borrow them, but Larry is my best friend, so I let him take it. He returned it yesterday, and it's ruined! There are big scratches on both sides. When I bought this record last year, it cost me $8.00. Now it's even more expensive. I think Larry owes me a new record. What do you think?

Bob

1. What did Larry ask Bob last week? _____
   _____

2. Why did Bob agree to do this? _____
   _____

3. What is the condition of Bob's record now? _____
   _____

4. What does Bob want? _____

5. What does the word *lend* in this letter mean? Circle the best answer.

   a. give for a while   b. take for a while   c. spend   d. break or ruin

6. What is your advice to Bob? Discuss your answer in class. Then read Dot's answer and tell why you agree or disagree. Dot's advice is below.

Dear Bob—

I agree that Larry owes you a new record, but you can't just say, "You ruined my album, give me $8.00 for a new one." Be friendly but firm. Tell him your problem. Show him the scratches and ask him to listen to the record with you. Remind him how you feel about your records. If he's a real friend, he should offer to replace this one for you.

Dot

Write About It

On your paper, write about a hobby or interest of yours. Explain what your hobby is and how (and when and where) you found out about it.

Skill Sharpeners 3—Unit 6

A Trip to the Moon: 1865

Use words from the Momory Bank to fill the blanks in the story. Write only one word in each blank. The same word can be used more than once, however. The first one is done for you.

Jules Verne is a famous French author who dreamed about wonderful machines and fantastic journeys. In 1865, Verne wrote ____a____ book about a trip to _____ moon. The name of the _____ was *From the Earth to the Moon.* The spaceship he described _____ very interesting. There were three "astronauts" in the spaceship, two Americans and _____ Frenchman. The _____ kept chickens in the ship for food! _____ beds they used were very comfortable, _____ they cooked their meals on _____ gas stove!

The men reached the _____ in 97 hours, 13 minutes _____ 20 seconds after _____ had left the earth. When they landed on the _____, they made a mistake and couldn't leave _____ spaceship. That was a good thing _____ they didn't have any spacesuits!

Verne's books were very popular. _____ at that time _____ fascinated with scientific developments and Verne included many scientific facts. Today we call _____ like this "science fiction."

In 1865, _____ thought Verne's dreams _____ impossible. But one hundred years later, _____ were walking on the moon.

```
──────────── MEMORY BANK ────────────
  a          and        because    book       books      men        moon
  one        and        the        the        was        were
             people                they
```

Skill Sharpeners 3—Unit 7

67

A Trip to the Moon: 1969

Read the story. Use your dictionary for any words you are not sure of.

Have you been to the moon lately? This is a question your grandchildren might ask their friends. One hundred years ago, a trip to the moon was only a dream. One hundred years from now, a trip to the moon might be as common as a trip to the next state.

On July 20, 1969, the dream to land on the moon became a reality. Astronaut Neil Armstrong stepped out of the Apollo 11 spacecraft's lunar module and walked on the moon's rocky surface for 18 minutes. A television camera on the module permitted people from all over the earth to see a human's first step on the moon. Everyone heard Armstrong say, "That's one small step for man, one giant leap for mankind."

Astronaut Edwin Aldrin joined Armstrong for another 2½ hours. A third astronaut, Michael Collins, stayed in the spacecraft. Armstrong and Aldrin collected rocks and soil samples and set up instruments to record vibrations caused by moonquakes. They also placed an American flag on the moon. Then their lunar module took them back to the orbiting spacecraft, and they returned to earth at the speed of 25,000 miles an hour.

The three astronauts couldn't eat regular food; they had to eat dehydrated (dried) food which didn't need refrigeration. And there were no gas stoves or comfortable beds on the Apollo 11 spacecraft as there were on the imaginary spaceship described by Jules Verne. But this was not science fiction. This was the real thing! It was indeed, "one giant leap" for the human race.

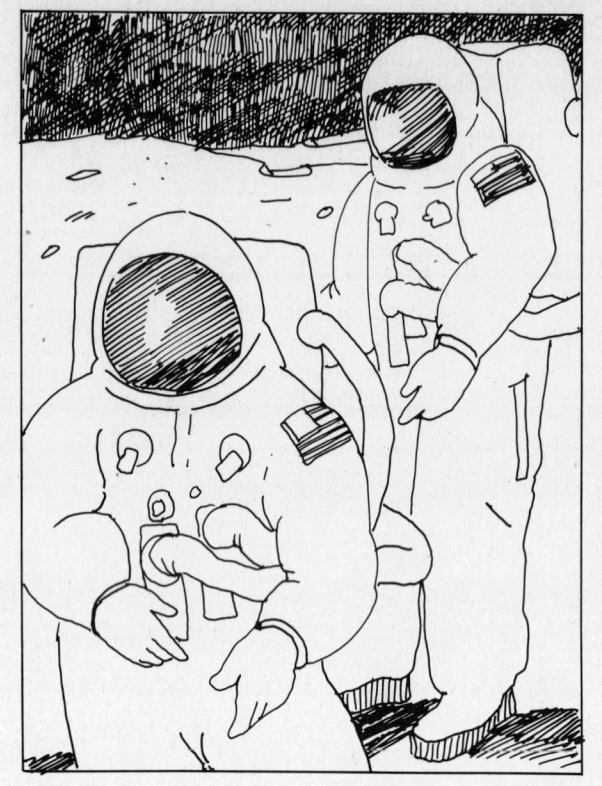

Read each sentence below and decide if it is true or false. Circle the T if it is true. Circle the F if it is false.

T F 1. One hundred years ago, people first traveled to the moon.

T F 2. The first person to walk on the moon was Edwin Aldrin.

T F 3. The astronauts walked on the moon for about three hours.

T F 4. The astronauts picked up soil and rock samples.

T F 5. Two astronauts walked on the moon.

T F 6. The astronauts returned to earth at 5,000 miles an hour.

T F 7. The astronauts ate fresh food.

T F 8. The spacecraft was the Apollo 11.

Word Skills: Irregular Plurals

Some plurals are difficult to form because of irregular spellings or because there are special rules for them. Look at the following rules for forming plurals. But be careful! There are many exceptions to these rules. Get into the habit of using your dictionary to check your work. It will give you the information you need about spelling irregularities and exceptions to the rules.

Rule 1: For words that end in a consonant followed by *y*, change the *y* to *i* and add *es* to form the plural. Example: *party, parties.*

Rule 2: For words that end in *sh, ch, x,* and *s,* add *es* to form the plural. Examples: *brush, brushes; church, churches; tax, taxes; kiss, kisses.*

Rule 3: For words that end in *f* or *fe,* change the *f* or *fe* to *v* and add *es.* Examples: *shelf, shelves; life, lives.* There are many exceptions to this rule.

Rule 4: Compound nouns form their plural by adding *s* to the most important word in the phrase. Example: *mother-in-law, mothers-in-law.*

Rule 5: For words that end in a consonant followed by *o,* add *es* to form the plural. Example: *potato, potatoes.* There are many exceptions to this rule, so check your dictionary.

Rule 6: Some words have special plural forms and do not take an *s* at all. Example: *man, men.*

Rule 7: Some words (mostly animal names) keep the same form in singular and plural. Example: *deer, deer.*

Make the following words plural. Use your dictionary.

1. thief _____
2. father-in-law _____
3. piano _____
4. penny _____
5. box _____
6. tooth _____
7. roof _____
8. tomato _____
9. mouse _____
10. scarf _____
11. moose _____
12. monkey _____
13. wife _____
14. foot _____
15. silo _____
16. wolf _____
17. sheep _____
18. chief _____
19. half _____
20. woman _____
21. pony _____
22. boss _____
23. wish _____
24. watch _____

Skill Sharpeners 3—Unit 7

Our Closest Neighbor

A. Read the story quickly to get a general idea of the subject. Then look at the Vocabulary Highlights. These words are underlined in the story. Be sure you understand the meaning of each word as it is used in the story. Check in the dictionary if you are unsure. Remember, some words have more than one meaning. Write down the meanings of the words that are new to you.

Vocabulary Highlights

distance	instruments
crater	shuttle
plain	refueling
shine	galaxies
mankind	universe

B. Now read the story again. Use the dictionary if there are other words you do not understand.

The Moon

The moon is our closest neighbor in the sky. It is only 239,000 miles away from us. Of course, that seems very far, but compared to the <u>distance</u> the Earth is from the sun or some of the other planets, it isn't much at all.

The moon is the Earth's satellite. It revolves or travels around the Earth. There are mountains, <u>craters</u>, and <u>plains</u> on the moon. Some of the moon's mountains are 15,000 feet high. The craters are large holes in the surface of the moon. The plains are gray, flat areas. Galileo, one of the first scientists to use a telescope to observe the moon, called the plains "seas" and "oceans."

The temperature on the moon can get as hot as 260°F. at noon and colder than 200°F. at night. During the day the sun <u>shines</u> on the moon. At night "earth-shine" lights up the moon. There is no air and no water on the moon. Scientists say that there never has been any life on the moon.

We learned a lot about the moon in 1959. Sputnik, a Soviet (Russian) space satellite, was the first to photograph the moon close up. Soon American rockets were traveling close to the moon. In July of 1969 the first human being walked on the moon. Neil Armstrong, an American, was the lucky person. He called his first step on the moon, "a small step for man; a giant step for <u>mankind</u>." Armstrong and Edwin Aldrin picked up rocks and dirt from the moon and left recording <u>instruments</u> there.

American scientists believe that a trip to the moon is just the beginning of space exploration. They have developed the space <u>shuttle</u>, a rocket ship that can travel long distances, land, and after <u>refueling</u> take off again. Scientists want to send spaceships to other planets and other <u>galaxies</u>. Their goal is to explore the whole <u>universe</u>.

(Go on to the next page.)

70   Skill Sharpeners 3—Unit 7

C. **Circle the answer that best completes the sentence.**

The American government paid more attention to its space program in 1960 because

a. it wanted to know more about the moon.
b. the moon is our closest neighbor.
c. there is no air or water on the moon.
d. the Soviet Union sent its sputnik into space in 1959.

D. **Use a word from the Vocabulary Highlights to complete each of these sentences.**

1. I love to go out at night and see the stars _____.

2. The _____ from the earth to the sun is 93,000,000 miles.

3. I hope that there is peace for all _____ in the future.

4. The crew is _____ the plane before it takes off again.

5. There are several _____ in the universe.

E. **Use separate paper to write answers to these questions.**

1. How far is the moon from the earth?
2. How high are the mountains on the moon?
3. What are craters?
4. What did Galileo call the moon's plains?
5. What is the moon's hottest temperature?
6. How cold can the temperature get on the moon?
7. Why do scientists say there is no life on the moon?
8. What nation first photographed the moon close up?
9. Who was the first person to walk on the moon?
10. When did the first person walk on the moon?
11. What did that person say about the first step on the moon?
12. What did the astronauts pick up on the moon?
13. What did they leave behind?
14. Where else do scientists want to send spaceships?
15. What is the goal of these scientists?

F. **Number these events in the order in which they happened.**

_____ Armstrong and Aldrin walked on the moon.

_____ Galileo observed the moon with a telescope.

_____ American scientists developed the space shuttle.

_____ Russians took the first close-up pictures of the moon.

_____ American spaceships traveled close to the moon.

G. The story says that it is very hot on the moon "at noon," and very cold "at night." What is a lunar (moon) day? What is a lunar night? How long is each of these? How are they related to what we call a full moon, a new moon, etc.? On your paper write a paragraph or paragraphs answering these questions. Use an encyclopedia if you need to, but write your paragraph(s) in your own words.

Skill Sharpeners 3—Unit 7

Library Catalog Cards

A library card catalog is a complete list, in card form, of the books owned by the library. To find out if the library owns a particular book, you look for that book in the catalog. To help you, the catalog has three kinds of cards for most books. There are author cards, which have the author's name at the top. There are title cards, which have the title of the book at the top. And there are subject cards, which have the subject of the book at the top. Often, all three cards are in the same set of catalog drawers. Sometimes, however, subject cards are in a separate set of drawers.

All the cards are filed alphabetically. Suppose you have a book called *Looking at the Moon*, by an author named John Adams. The author card will be filed with the A's. The title card will be filed with the L's. And the subject card will be filed with the M's (for Moon). If you look under the M's, you will find other books on the same subject written by different authors. If you look under the A's, you will find other books by the same author, perhaps on different subjects. If you look under the L's, you will find other books whose titles start with "Look" or "Looking."

All the cards give you complete information about the book, including its title, its author(s), its publisher, and its subject. They also give you information about where it is located in the library. A "call number" in the upper left-hand corner of the card identifies the section of the library where the book is kept.

Look at the list below. These are the top lines from some catalog cards. **Tell which kind of card each one is. Write "author card," "title card," or "subject card" next to each one.**

1. RAILROADS _____
2. E.B. White _____
3. *Huckleberry Finn* _____
4. *Moby Dick* _____
5. PILGRIMS _____
6. CIVIL WAR _____
7. Madeleine L'Engle _____
8. F. Scott Fitzgerald _____
9. *The Call of the Wild* _____
10. SLAVERY _____
11. John Steinbeck _____
12. *For Whom the Bell Tolls* _____
13. *The Groucho Letters* _____
14. NEW YORK CITY _____
15. Ellen Goodman _____
16. *A Room of One's Own* _____
17. MOVIES _____
18. WITCHCRAFT _____
19. Emily Dickinson _____
20. *Pride and Prejudice* _____

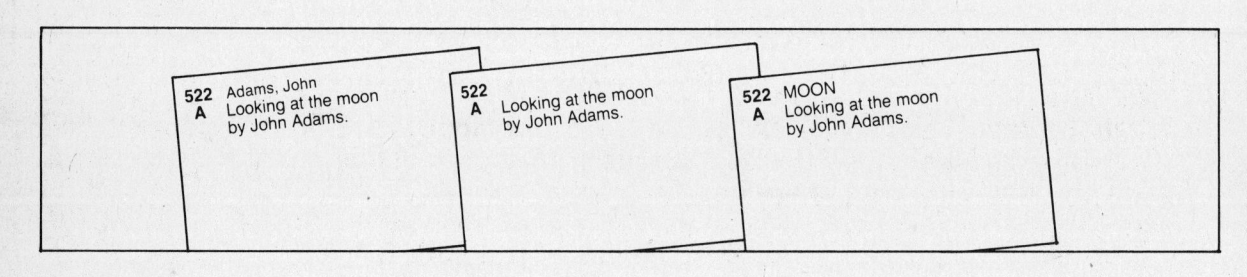

```
522  Adams, John
A    Looking at the moon
     by John Adams.

522  Looking at the moon
A    by John Adams.

522  MOON
A    Looking at the moon
     by John Adams.
```

Skill Objective: Using the card catalog Read and discuss the introduction together, then assign the exercises. Extension Activities: Have students use the card catalog to answer these questions: 1. Where are the subject cards filed in your library? 2. How many books can you find about railroads, the Pilgrims, movies, witchcraft? 3. Which books does your library have by the authors on this page? 4. Does your library have the books listed on this page? Write down the call numbers and locate the books on the shelves.

The Future with "Will"

One way to talk about things that are going to happen in the future is to use the verb *will*. Look at the examples below.

I will graduate
He will ride
She will study
It will rain

You will leave
We will arrive
They will stay

You can use *will* with many future expressions such as the following:

next week
next month

next year
in a year

in a few days (weeks, months)
tomorrow

A. Read the following paragraph and follow the instructions.

We and our children will see many changes in the world in the next fifty years, just as our parents and grandparents have seen many changes in the past fifty years. Here are some of the kinds of changes some people think we will see:

1. We will drive electric cars.
2. We will find a cure for cancer and other diseases.
3. We will use solar energy in all our homes.
4. We will all have our own computers.
5. We will visit the moon for a vacation.
6. We will eat factory-made food.
7. We will travel by monorail in the cities.

What else do you think we will do in the next fifty years? Add three changes of your own.

8. _____
9. _____
10. _____

B. Now work with a classmate asking and answering questions from the ten changes above. Use the following model:

—Do you think we will drive electric cars in the next fifty years?

—Yes, I think we will drive electric cars.
                or
—No, I don't think we will drive electric cars.

C. On your paper, write answers to these questions. Use complete sentences with *will*.

1. When will you graduate from high school?
2. How old will you be on your next birthday?
3. What will you do this weekend?
4. Will you get a job or will you go to college after you graduate?
5. How old will you be when you get married?
6. When will your next school vacation begin?

Skill Sharpeners 3—Unit 7

Dear Dot

Dear Dot—

My sister Luisa keeps a diary. I know I was wrong, but one night when she left it on top of her desk I read it. Now I don't know what to do. Luisa met a boy two weeks ago, and he wants to marry her. She said no, but she wrote in her diary that every day she wants to go off with him a little bit more. You see, she's not happy at home. My parents nag her all the time because she gets bad grades in school. My problem is that if I ask my sister any questions, she will know that I read her diary. If I tell my mother, my sister will be very angry. What should I do?

Snoopy

1. Where did Luisa leave her diary? _____

2. What is Luisa's secret? _____

3. Why does she want to leave home? _____

4. What is Snoopy's problem? _____

5. What does the word *nag* mean in this letter? Circle the best answer.

   a. call and write   b. criticize constantly   c. kiss and praise   d. old horse

6. What is your advice to Snoopy? Discuss your answer in class. Then read Dot's answer and tell why you agree or disagree. Dot's advice is below.

Dear Snoopy—

You're going to have to tell your sister that you read her diary. She is going to be angry, but she will probably also be glad finally to have someone she can talk to about her problem. Don't tell your mother before you talk to your sister. People sometimes use a diary just to "blow off steam." Your sister may not feel as strongly about your home and your parents as she did in her diary. You're right, you were wrong to read your sister's diary. Now you know why.

Dot

Write About It

Write a page in a diary. Make it a fantasy that you wish would come true. Begin your page like this: "Dear Diary, A fantastic thing happened to me today . . ."

Skill Sharpeners 3—Unit 7

Thank You

When someone gives you something, you say "Thank you." Sometimes, however, a letter or note is expected. "Thank-you" notes are usually sent

    a. when someone sends you a gift—for example, a birthday or Christmas present;

    b. when you have visited someone—for example, for a weekend or a vacation.

Here are two different kinds of "thank-you" notes:

> February 8
>
> Dear Carolina,
>
> The scarf you sent to me is just beautiful. It's just the color I needed to go with my gray coat, and it's so soft! Thank you so much. It was sweet of you to remember my birthday.
>
>   Love,
>   Lucy

> May 16
>
> Dear Anh,
>
> I had a wonderful time at your home last weekend. I was a little nervous at first, but everyone was so friendly I felt right at home. Thank you very much for having me.
>
>   Sincerely,
>   Ngoc

Notice that the notes are short and that they are written by hand, not typewritten. "Thank-you" notes should be sent promptly, within a month for gifts, and within a week after your return for visits.

Practice writing a thank-you note. Use the space below. Write your note to an aunt who has just sent you a sweater for your birthday. Or, if you have just received a gift or come back from a visit, write a note thanking the person who gave you the gift or asked you to visit.

Skill Sharpeners 3—Unit 8

Call the Doctor!

Most people are healthy most of the time, but now and then people do not feel well. Some people have serious illnesses or conditions, some have temporary sicknesses that are less serious, and some have diseases that they have "caught" from other people. Look at the three lists below. Use your dictionary or an encyclopedia to find out about each of the items on the lists.

Illness/Condition	Sickness	Communicable Diseases
diabetes	flu (virus)	chicken pox
heart trouble	fever	German measles
cancer	headache, earache, backache, etc.	measles
tuberculosis		mumps
allergy	upset stomach	scarlet fever
asthma	diarrhea	

A. Look at the list of conditions at the left. Draw a line from each condition to the symptoms (the way you feel or the effects of the condition) at the right. The first one is done for you. Use your dictionary or an encyclopedia to help you.

1. headache
2. allergy
3. chicken pox
4. fever
5. upset stomach
6. diabetes
7. heart trouble
8. flu

a. you have a temperature of 102°F
b. you feel like throwing up your food
c. your body can't use sugar and you need insulin shots
d. you have a headache, sore throat, fever, earache, and cold
e. you sneeze from dust, flowers, and animals
f. children get red spots on their bodies
g. your heart is weak
h. your head hurts

B. Different kinds of doctors take care of different kinds of diseases or conditions. Use words from the Memory Bank to complete each of these sentences. Use your dictionary if you need to.

1. When a woman is going to have a baby, she goes to a(n) _____.
2. When the baby is born, she takes it to a(n) _____.
3. A family doctor who treats common illnesses is a(n) _____.
4. If you have a toothache, you go to a(n) _____.
5. If you have to have your appendix removed, you go to a(n) _____.
6. If you are having trouble with your eyes, you go to a(n) _____.
7. People who are feeling depressed can go to a(n) _____.

---- **MEMORY BANK** ----

| dentist | general practitioner | obstetrician | ophthalmologist |
| pediatrician | psychiatrist | surgeon | |

C. On your paper, write the names of other kinds of doctors and tell what they do. Use an encyclopedia to find this information.

Skill Sharpeners 3—Unit 8

In the Drugstore

Look at the picture of the drugstore and the list of products it sells.

HEALTH	COSMETICS	HYGIENE	OTHER
aspirin	make-up	shampoo	newspapers
Band-Aids	lipstick	deodorant	magazines
cough drops	powder	toothpaste	greeting cards
rubbing alcohol	mascara	hair color	stationery
antacid tablets	perfume	combs	
	skin cream	razor blades	

Use words from the box above to complete the sentences.

1. Mike had a headache, so he bought some _____.

2. I have to wash my hair. I need some _____.

3. Maria cut her finger. She needs a _____.

4. Henry needs paper to write to his family. He will buy some _____.

5. My aunt's birthday is next week. I want to send her a _____.

6. Mr. Rivera is growing a beard, so he won't need any _____.

7. To find an apartment, you look in the Real Estate section of the _____.

8. You need _____ to brush your teeth.

9. When Linda's skin gets very dry, she uses some _____.

10. If your stomach is upset, you may want to buy some _____.

Skill Sharpeners 3—Unit 8

Follow the Directions

When you take any kind of medicine, it is important to follow the directions for that medicine. Your medicine may be either something prescribed by a doctor and supplied to you by a pharmacist in a drugstore or something that anyone can buy from a drugstore counter.

A. When a doctor believes you need a special kind of medicine, he or she writes a *prescription*. You take the prescription to the pharmacist who gives you the medicine. The label on the container tells you what the medicine is and how often you should take it.

Look at this label. Use it to answer the questions.

> **STONE PHARMACY**
> Jason Stone, Reg. Pharm.
> Tel. 898-0225
>
> No. 806-943   Date 7/2/81
>
> Catherine Cook   Pen VK
> 250 mg
>
> One tablet every 4 hours.
>
> Dr. Morton

1. Who is the medicine for? _____
2. Is Jason Stone the doctor or the pharmacist? _____
3. What is the number of the prescription? _____
4. Pen VK is penicillin. What is penicillin? _____
5. Is Pen VK a liquid? _____
6. How often does Catherine have to take her medicine? _____
7. What is the name of the drugstore? _____

B. Most medicines that you buy from the drugstore counter have directions on the container. **Look at this set of directions from an aspirin bottle and use it to answer the questions.**

1. Why do people take aspirin? _____

> Aspirin is used for relief of simple headache and for temporary relief of minor arthritic pain, the discomfort and fever of colds or "flu," menstrual cramps, muscular aches from fatigue, and toothache. Dosage: 2 tablets every four hours as needed. Do not exceed 12 tablets in 24 hours unless directed by physician. For children 6–12, one-half dose. Under 6, consult physician. **Warning: Keep this and all medicines out of children's reach. In case of accidental overdose, consult physician immediately. Caution:** If pain persists for more than 10 days or redness is present or in arthritic or rheumatic conditions affecting children under 12, consult a physician immediately. Do not take without consulting a physician if under medical care. Consult a dentist for toothache promptly. **Active ingredient:** Aspirin, 5 gr.
> STORE AT ROOM TEMPERATURE

2. What is the recommended adult dosage? _____

3. What is the recommended dosage for children aged 6 to 12? _____

4. What should parents of a child under 6 do before they give their child aspirin? _____

5. Should you keep this bottle in the refrigerator? _____

Skill Sharpeners 3—Unit 8

Word Skills: Categories

A good way to test your word knowledge is to complete categories of words. A category is a group of similar things, in this case words. **After each category name below, write five words that belong in the category. Use any words that fit the category name. Use your dictionary or other books if you need to.** The first one is done for you.

1. Colors	red	orange	green	blue	yellow
2. Clothing					
3. Vegetables					
4. Fruit					
5. Cities					
6. States					
7. Countries					
8. School Subjects					
9. Large Animals					
10. Small Animals					
11. Months					
12. Sports					
13. Occupations					
14. Family Members					
15. Machines					
16. Rooms in a House					
17. Kinds of Buildings					
18. Weather Words					
19. Motor Vehicles					
20. Illnesses					

Skill Objectives: Classifying, reviewing vocabulary. After students have completed this page, ask volunteers to name the different items listed by members of the class for each category. Keep a tally or list of all the words they have listed after each category.

Skill Sharpeners 3—Unit 8

Stormy Weather!

A. Read the story quickly to get a general idea of the subject. Then look at the Vocabulary Highlights. These words are underlined in the story. Be sure you understand the meaning of each word as it is used in the story. Check in the dictionary if you are unsure. Remember, some words have more than one meaning. Write down the meanings of the words that are new to you.

Vocabulary Highlights

meteorologists	occur
define	blizzards
dangerous	cloudbursts
hurricane	snowdrifts
tornado	sleet
damage	hail

B. Now read the story again. Use the dictionary if there are other words you do not understand.

Weather

Bad weather is like bad news; it comes in many forms. When most people think of bad weather, they think of rain and snow. There are many kinds of bad weather, however. Meteorologists, people who study weather, have named and defined all of the different kinds of bad weather.

Perhaps the most dangerous weather situations are hurricanes and tornadoes. A hurricane is a great windstorm that covers hundreds of square miles for as long as 24 hours at a time. A hurricane brings along a lot of rain as well as very strong winds. Hurricanes can do millions of dollars worth of damage to property. Hurricanes occur most often in the summertime.

A tornado is a whirling windstorm. It doesn't have the rain of a hurricane but it moves very fast and does a lot of damage. Tornadoes have destroyed whole towns in the midwestern part of the United States. In 1925, in the southern central part of the United States, 689 people were killed by a tornado that lasted only three hours. Because they look like great twisted ropes of cloud, tornadoes are often called "twisters."

Blizzards and cloudbursts aren't as dangerous as hurricanes and tornadoes, but they are certainly bad weather. A cloudburst is a very heavy rainstorm that falls for a short period of time. The record for a cloudburst is one and a half inches of rain in one minute in Guadeloupe in the Caribbean. A blizzard is a snowstorm with a strong wind. The strong winds of a blizzard blow the snow everywhere. Driving a car becomes very dangerous, because you cannot see anything in front of you. The hills of snow, called snowdrifts, can block roads and trap people inside their houses for days.

Hailstorms and sleet storms are other bad weather situations. Hail is made of balls of ice, called hailstones. Hail forms when raindrops freeze high in the sky. When it hails, people run for protection. The icy balls can really hurt! Sleet is rain that freezes as it falls. Sleet isn't as large as hail and doesn't hurt as much as hail, but it is best to stay inside during either of these storms.

You can hear all these words if you watch the national weather reports on network television news programs. Weather forecasters on these programs tell about weather all over the country. Tune in several evenings and you'll hear all about weather!

(Go on to the next page.)

C. **Circle the answer that best completes the sentence.**

A hurricane is different from a tornado because

  a. it carries fast winds.
  b. it happens in the United States.
  c. it causes a lot of damage.
  d. it brings a lot of rain.

D. **Use a word from the Vocabulary Highlights to complete each of these sentences.**

  1. It is _____ to drive faster than the speed limit.
  2. The accident caused a lot of _____ to Helen's van.
  3. Miguel's father is a _____ at the television station.
  4. It is difficult to _____ the word "weather."
  5. Small earthquakes _____ every day somewhere in the world.

E. **Use separate paper to write answers to these questions.**

  1. What is a meteorologist?
  2. What is a hurricane?
  3. What is a tornado?
  4. Where have tornadoes done a lot of damage?
  5. What is a cloudburst?
  6. What is a blizzard?
  7. Why is it dangerous to drive in a blizzard?
  8. What is a snowdrift?
  9. What is hail?
  10. What is sleet?

F. Weather maps are issued by the National Weather Service every day. They show the weather in different parts of the country. This map shows the midcontinental United States one February day. **Look at the key at the top of the map and answer these questions.**

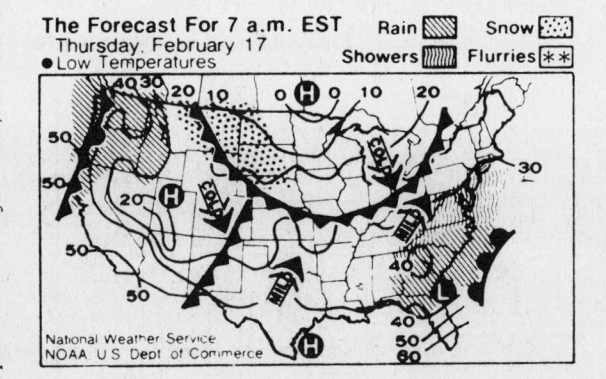

  1. What is the weather like in the northwest part of the country? _____
  2. What is the weather like in the Southeast? _____
  3. Is it snowing anywhere? If so, where? _____
  4. The numbers stand for temperatures. What part of the country is very cold? _____
  5. What part of the country is quite warm? _____

G. Use an encyclopedia to find out what the other symbols on the weather map mean. Then write a paragraph on your paper telling as much as you can about the weather on this February day.

Skill Sharpeners 3—Unit 8

Dear Dot

Dear Dot—

My parents are divorced. I live with my mother most of the year and I spend the summer vacations with my father. I like seeing my father, but it is boring spending so much time at his house. He works a lot, and I am in the house alone. Last summer my friends at home built a terrific club house and spent a lot of nights sleeping outside. They had a great time, and they sent me letters telling me about all their adventures. I don't want to miss another summer with my friends, but I don't want to hurt my father's feelings, either. What can I do?

Sonny

1. Where does Sonny spend his summer vacations? _____

2. What did Sonny's friends do last summer? _____

3. How did Sonny know about his friends' activities? _____

4. What does the word *boring* mean in this letter? Circle the best answer.

   a. not interested   b. fun   c. old-fashioned   d. not interesting

5. What is your advice to Sonny? Discuss your answer in class. Then read Dot's answer and tell why you agree or disagree. Dot's advice is below.

Dear Sonny—

You are going to have to talk this over with both your parents. If you stay home, is it all right with your mother? If you cut your summer vacations short, or don't go at all, can you see your father at some other time during the year? You have a lot of serious thinking to do before you make your decision. Don't miss out on an opportunity to spend time with your father for a few nights of camping. It might not be as much fun as it sounds in the letters.

Dot

Write About It

On your paper, write about a difficult decision that you have had to make. Tell what the possible choices were and which one you chose. Tell how you felt about your choice after you had made it. Do you have regrets? Are you satisfied that you chose wisely?

What Did She Tell You?

Complete the conversations. The first one and the fourth one are done for you.

1. "Please wash the dishes." / "What did she tell you?" / "She told me to wash the dishes."

2. "Please make your bed." / "What did he tell you?" / "He _____"

3. "Please mow the lawn!" / "What did she tell you?" / "She _____"

4. "Set the table." / "What did he ask you to do?" / "He asked me to set the table."

5. "Mail this letter, please." / "What did she ask you to do?" / "She _____"

6. "Do your homework!" / "What did they tell you?" / "They _____"

7. "Meet me in the cafeteria!" / "What did she want you to do?" / "She _____"

Skill Objective: Reporting speech
Write commands on pieces of paper. *Read your book. Go away. Hurry up.* etc. Write on the board, *What did he/she tell you?* Have a volunteer whisper a written command to you. The class will ask, "What did he/she tell you?" Model the answer, "She told me to. . . ." Have students come up in pairs. Hand a command to one student and practice these structures. Assign the page as independent work.

Skill Sharpeners 3—Unit 9

How Long?

I have been sleeping	He has been sleeping		hours
You have been sleeping	She has been sleeping	for ___	weeks
We have been sleeping	It has been sleeping		days
They have been sleeping			years

These verbs are in the present perfect continuous tense. The present perfect continuous is used for activities that *started sometime in the* PAST *but continue up to the* PRESENT. **Look at the example. Use it as a model to answer the "how long" questions.**

Example: I started studying English one year ago. (PAST)
I am studying English now. (PRESENT)
How long have you been studying English?

I have been studying English for one year.

1. Cathy started doing her homework one hour ago. (PAST)
   She is doing her homework now. (PRESENT)
   How long has she been doing her homework?

   _____

2. It started raining two hours ago.
   It is raining now.
   How long has it been raining?

   _____

3. Tom started taking guitar lessons two years ago.
   Tom is taking guitar lessons now.
   How long has Tom been taking guitar lessons?

   _____

4. Linda and John started cooking dinner half an hour ago.
   They are cooking dinner now.
   How long have they been cooking dinner?

   _____

5. You and your brother started arguing ten minutes ago.
   You are both arguing now.
   How long have you and your brother been arguing?

   _____

6. Mrs. Tomasino started working at the bank five years ago.
   She is working at the bank today.
   How long has Mrs. Tomasino been working at the bank?

   _____

7. The baby started sleeping one hour ago.
   The baby is sleeping now.
   How long has the baby been sleeping?

   _____

For and Since

Use *for* with general time words that describe a period or length of time, but don't give an exact date or time when an action started. For example:

I have been living here . . .
   for a few years.
   for a month.
   for a couple of weeks.
   for three hours.
   for all my life.

Use *sin[ce]* . . .
tell wh[en]
phrase[s]
starte[d]

I hav[e]
   sin[ce]
   s[ince]
   since M[onday]
   since 6:00 P.M.
   since I was a young g[irl].

Using the rules in the boxes above, complete the following sentences using *for* or *since*.

1. I have been living here _____ six weeks.
2. Tom has been working at the store _____ a year.
3. The girls have been listening to the records _____ 3:30.
4. That castle has been standing _____ several centuries.
5. I have been waiting for you _____ 9:00.
6. Sally has been reading that book _____ three weeks.
7. You have been talking on the telephone _____ two hours.
8. My friend has been writing to me _____ July 3rd.
9. James has been living with the Medinas _____ a couple of months.
10. Marco has been driving _____ he was 16 years old.
11. The children have been playing _____ several hours.
12. We have been sitting in this class _____ 45 minutes.
13. Mr. Jackson has been teaching _____ he graduated from college.
14. I have been calling _____ Wednesday.
15. It has been raining _____ almost a month.
16. The baby has been crying _____ ten minutes.
17. Paula and Simon have been dancing _____ 8:30.
18. Regina has been studying for her exam _____ two weeks.
19. I have been asking that same question _____ a long time.
20. We have been looking for a good restaurant _____ 12:00.
21. The secretary has been typing _____ 3½ hours.
22. She has been working at the bank _____ last summer.
23. Robert has been sailing _____ he was a young boy.
24. Jacqueline has been painting pictures _____ six years.

Skill Sharpeners 3—Unit 9

and How Many?

sentences to answer the questions. The first one is done for you.

Fran is a truck driver. She started driving a truck last year and she is driving a truck today.

How long has she been *driving* a truck? <u>She has been driving a truck for one year.</u> (TIME)

How many miles has she *driven* in the past year? <u>She has driven 200,000 miles in the past year.</u> (QUANTITY)

1983
200,000 miles

Lisa is a writer. She started writing books in 1980, and she is writing today.

How long has she been *writing* books? _____

How many books has she *written* since 1980? _____

1980
3 books

Henry and Roberta are teachers. They both started teaching in 1963 and they are teaching today.

How long have they been *teaching*? _____

How many students have they *taught* since 1963? _____

1963
1600 students

We are real estate salesmen. We started selling houses in 1958. We are selling houses today.

How long have we been *selling* homes? _____

How many houses have we *sold* since 1958? _____

1958
401 homes

I am a shoemaker. I started making shoes in 1925. I am making shoes today.

How long have I been *making* shoes? _____

How many pairs of shoes have I *made* since 1925? _____

1925
3000 pairs

Skill Objective: Comparing present perfect continuous and present perfect. Read the first example with the class. Have a volunteer explain why the present perfect continuous is used in the first question and the present perfect in the second question. Assign the page as independent work. Extension Activity: Have students draw portraits and write similar "stories" and questions about other professionals (a surgeon, two cooks, an explorer, etc.) Their classmates can read the stories and answer the questions.

86

Skill Sharpeners 3—Unit 9

Martha Miller

Last month, Martha Miller won $10,000 in the state lottery. She has decided to take a vacation to Paris, France. Paris is a place she has always wanted to visit. She has been very busy lately making plans for her trip. She plans to leave next month.

Martha has been calling a few travel agents. In the past month she has called three agents. She wants to know more about Paris, so she has been reading a few books about that city. In the past month, she has read two books.

Martha also wants to be able to speak the language, so she has been taking French lessons at the university. In the past month, she has taken eight lessons. She has been shopping for some new clothes, too. She has shopped in some of the best stores in her city. She has also been making new clothes. She has already made a skirt, and a blouse.

As you can see, Martha has been having a good time getting ready for her trip. Sometimes, getting ready for a vacation is half the fun!

A. Write questions about the story to fit the answers at the right. The first one is done for you.

1. How much _did Martha Miller win_ ? She won $10,000.
2. Where _____ ? She has decided to go to France.
3. Why _____ ? She has always wanted to go there.
4. When _____ ? She plans to leave in a month.
5. Who _____ ? She's been calling a few travel agents.
6. How many _____ ? She's called three agents so far.
7. What _____ ? She's been reading a few books about France.
8. How many _____ ? She has read two books so far.
9. Why _____ ? She wants to know more about Paris.
10. Where _____ ? She has been taking French at the university.
11. Has _____ ? Yes, she has.
12. What _____ ? She's made a skirt and a blouse.
13. Has _____ ? No, she hasn't.
14. _____ ? _____

B. On your paper, write five true or false statements about the story. For example: Martha Miller won $50,000 (false). She is going to take a vacation in Paris (true).

Skill Sharpeners 3—Unit 9

An Important Science

A. Read the story quickly to get a general idea of the subject. Then look at the Vocabulary Highlights. These words are underlined in the story. Be sure you understand the meaning of each word as it is used in the story. Check in the dictionary if you are unsure. Remember, some words have more than one meaning. Write down the meanings of the words that are new to you.

Vocabulary Highlights

complicated	split
principles	atoms
matter	examine
molecules	substance
attract	combine
collection	rusty
escape	sour

B. Now read the story again. Use the dictionary if there are other words you do not understand.

Chemistry

Many students feel that chemistry is a difficult subject. They are so afraid of the challenge of chemistry that they don't take the time to learn anything about it. It is true that chemistry is a <u>complicated</u> subject, but there are some ideas and <u>principles</u> of chemistry that everyone can and should understand. They are:

1. All <u>matter</u> (all things) is made up of small separate particles called <u>molecules</u>.
2. Molecules move very fast and they are always moving.
3. Molecules <u>attract</u> each other.

Let's look at an example of these three rules. A bottle of ammonia is a <u>collection</u> of ammonia molecules. If you open a bottle of ammonia in a closed room, the smell is everywhere in the room. Why? Some molecules of ammonia (remember molecules are very small and you can't see them) have <u>escaped</u> from the bottle and are flying through the air. They cause the smell. Why don't all of the molecules fly out of the bottle? Remember rule number three. Molecules attract each other. Most of the molecules don't escape because they are attracted to, or pulled toward, each other.

Molecules are not the smallest particles of matter. Scientists can <u>split</u> the molecule into smaller particles called <u>atoms</u>. Chemistry is the study of molecules and atoms. Chemists <u>examine</u> different <u>substances</u> and find out about their molecules and atoms. Chemists <u>combine</u> molecules of one substance with molecules of another. They want to see what changes take place.

Why does a nail, left outside, get <u>rusty</u>? Why does bread rise when you bake it? Why does milk get <u>sour</u>? These are all chemical changes. If you want to know what causes these chemical changes, why not try a chemistry course? Chemistry is complicated but it is also rewarding. It explains many of the occurrences of day-to-day living.

(Go on to the next page.)

Skill Sharpeners 3—Unit 9

C. Circle the answer that best completes the sentence.

According to this article, a sliced onion makes you cry because

    a. the knife splits the atoms.
    b. the molecules attract each other.
    c. some molecules escape and reach the eyes.
    d. the molecules move very fast.

D. Use a word from the Vocabulary Highlights to complete each of these sentences.

1. Ramon has an interesting _____ of butterflies.
2. I can't understand these directions; they're too _____.
3. The milk doesn't taste good; I think it's _____.
4. Two prisoners tried to _____ from jail last week.
5. Artists _____ colors to make new and different shades.

E. Use separate paper to write answers to these questions.

1. Why are many students afraid of chemistry?
2. What is the smallest particle of matter mentioned in the story?
3. What do chemists do?
4. Why do chemists combine molecules of different substances?
5. Why is chemistry rewarding?

F. Certain things cause certain other things to happen. Look at the causes at the left. Find the effect at the right that goes with each cause, and write its letter in the blank for that cause. Use your dictionary for words you don't know.

1. too many automobiles in a city _____	a. damage and destruction
2. drinking too much alcohol _____	b. sourness
3. vitamin deficiency _____	c. temporary pain relief
4. tornado _____	d. drunkenness
5. taking aspirin tablets _____	e. sickness and body malfunction
6. leaving a nail outdoors _____	f. air pollution
7. leaving milk out of the refrigerator _____	g. rust

G. Find out what the word *synthetic* means. What does this have to do with chemistry? Use an encyclopedia to find out some of the common things around you that have been developed by chemists. Take notes, then write a paragraph telling the facts you have learned in your own words.

Skill Sharpeners 3—Unit 9

Word Skills: Category Labels

In the last unit, you listed words that belonged in particular categories. In this activity, the words are listed for you, but you have to supply names or labels for the categories. Look at each list below. Decide how the words on the list are the same, and think of a word or phrase that names or labels the list. Write the word in the blank. Use your dictionary or other books if you need to. The first list is labeled for you.

1. _____*languages*_____ Spanish, Chinese, Italian, Vietnamese, English
2. _____ Monopoly, chess, checkers, dominoes, Scrabble
3. _____ piano, guitar, drums, saxophone, string bass
4. _____ lily, petunia, rose, daisy, daffodil
5. _____ sofa, chair, table, bed, dresser
6. _____ wash clothes, iron, do dishes, empty trash, sweep
7. _____ Christmas, New Year, Independence Day, Thanksgiving
8. _____ poodle, collie, dalmation, German shepherd, spaniel
9. _____ penny, nickel, dime, quarter, half-dollar
10. _____ novel, dictionary, encyclopedia, Bible, atlas
11. _____ Saturn, Neptune, Pluto, Mars, Mercury
12. _____ dog, cat, fish, bird, hamster
13. _____ sparrow, robin, blue jay, eagle, pigeon
14. _____ Carson City, Austin, Sacramento, Albany, Helena
15. _____ trout, salmon, cod, shark, mackerel
16. _____ ant, grasshopper, fly, bee, cockroach
17. _____ North America, South America, Europe, Africa, Asia
18. _____ Capricorn, Leo, Aries, Pisces, Libra
19. _____ Mary, Ruth, Betty, Lisa, Rita
20. _____ bacon, lettuce, and tomato; ham and cheese; tuna fish; peanut butter and jelly; grilled cheese

Dear Dot

Dear Dot—

I bought my girlfriend an expensive necklace for her birthday. She liked it, but she wouldn't accept it. She told me that her mother taught her not to accept such expensive presents from someone she was not engaged to. I am very disappointed. I want her to have this necklace, and I don't care about some silly rule of etiquette that says otherwise. Dot, does that old rule really matter anymore?

Diamond Jim

1. What did Jim buy his girlfriend for her birthday? _____

2. Why didn't his girlfriend accept the gift? _____

3. How does Jim feel about the situation? _____

4. What does Jim want? _____

5. What does the word *silly* mean in this letter? Circle the best answer.

    a. foolish   b. old   c. friendly   d. careful

6. What is your advice to Jim? Discuss your answer in class. Then read Dot's answer and tell why you agree or disagree. Dot's advice is below.

Dear Jim—

That old rule matters to your girlfriend and her family, and so it should matter to you, too. Be gracious and respect their wishes. If and when you and your girlfriend get engaged, you can give her expensive gifts. But don't embarrass her by trying to force them on her now. This "silly rule," like most rules of etiquette, is based on good common sense. You don't want to make your girlfriend feel she owes you something, do you?

Dot

Write About It

Everyone learns certain rules of etiquette at home. On your paper, write a paragraph about some of the rules of conduct that are a part of your upbringing.

Skill Sharpeners 3—Unit 9

Something, Anything

Complete each of the sentences by filling each blank with one of the following words:

    some   any   anybody   somebody   anything   something

The first one is done for you.

1. She doesn't have _____*any*_____ money in her account.
2. There are _____ students from China in my class.
3. I don't think _____ has seen her recently.
4. There aren't _____ students in my class from Russia.
5. Shhh! I think I hear _____ in the next room.
6. _____ ate my lunch!
7. May I have _____ more tea, please.
8. I wanted to borrow _____ money from her but she said that she didn't have _____.
9. She never gives her poor cat _____ milk to drink.
10. The police asked me _____ questions but I didn't know _____.
11. I didn't have _____ milk, so I went to the store to buy _____.
12. I entered the room but I didn't see _____ so I left.
13. I thought I heard a noise in the next room but my wife didn't hear _____.
14. It's my mother's birthday tomorrow, so I have to go out and buy her _____.
15. There is _____ wrong with my bike.
16. Mr. Villalba never gives his wife _____ money.
17. The baby is hungry so I'm giving her _____ to eat.
18. David didn't want _____ to eat.
19. _____ just telephoned you; he's going to call back later.
20. I have _____ to tell you.

I Just Ate!

The word *just* has several meanings. One meaning of *just* is "recently in the past." It is used with the past tense or the present perfect tense. "I just ate" and "I have just eaten" both mean "I finished eating a few minutes ago." **Use the word *just* in your answers to the questions below.** The first two are done for you. Use them as models for the others.

1. Why is John upset?

   John is upset because his dog has just eaten part of the rug.

2. Why is Lisa happy?

   Lisa is happy because she just won $1000 in the lottery.

3. Why is Christina happy?

4. Why is Rolando upset?

5. Why is Mrs. Poleo mad?

6. Why is Alexis happy?

7. Why is Carla sad?

8. Why are Mr. and Mrs. Soto happy?

9. Why is Mr. Nguyen upset?

Skill Objective: Using *just* with present perfect and simple past. Whisper to a student, "Write on the board." Then ask, "What did s(he) just do?" If needed, prompt answer, "She just wrote on the board." Direct another student to erase the board and ask, "What has he just done?" If needed, provide additional situations for oral practice. Go over the first two items together. Point out that either the simple past or the present perfect can be used. Assign as independent work.

Skill Sharpeners 3—Unit 10

Using Reference Books

A reference book is a book designed to provide information on one or more subjects. Dictionaries and encyclopedias are reference books. There are many other kinds of reference books, too. Some of these are described below. **Look at the descriptions and use them to help you complete the page.**

Some Reference Books

Almanac: a yearly publication that includes lists, charts and tables, and summaries of information in many unrelated fields.
Atlas: a collection of maps; atlases often also include population statistics.
Book of Quotations: a listing of well-known quotations from authors, politicians, and other famous people. The quotations are indexed to make them easy to find.
Facts on File: a bimonthly summary of major stories in more than fifty United States and foreign newspapers. Complete indexes make stories easy to locate.
Thesaurus: a book of synonyms and antonyms.
Readers' Guide to Periodical Literature: an author/subject index of articles and stories in a large number of magazines published in the United States. It comes out twice a month (once a month in certain months).

Now look at the topics below. Tell which of the reference books described above you might use to find more information about the subject. Include the dictionary and encyclopedia. The first one is done for you.

1. the height of Mount Shasta — atlas (or almanac, encyclopedia)
2. synonyms for the word *run*
3. maps of the Central Plains states
4. riots in London last summer
5. who wrote "To be or not to be . . ."
6. the opposite of *careful*
7. recent developments in bilingual education
8. rainfall in Tokyo
9. antonyms for the word *happy*
10. source of "A penny saved is a penny earned."
11. current population of Senegal
12. a series of recent murders in New York City
13. another word meaning *laugh*
14. articles about track competition
15. last month's elections in Honduras
16. the origin and different meanings of *rich*
17. all magazine articles by John Updike
18. maps of all the countries of Europe
19. brief biographies of the Presidents
20. the origin and history of the metric system

It's Your Choice

A. In each sentence, circle the correct verb form. The first one is done for you.

1. I have just ((written)-wrote) to my friend Jerry.
2. Dick has (drove-driven) 200 miles in the past three hours.
3. My father (spoken-spoke) to the principal about my problem.
4. Janice (broke-broken) her leg last week.
5. Maria has already (saw-seen) that movie.
6. The teacher (chose-chosen) Ali to be the group leader.
7. Have you ever (broke-broken) your arm?
8. My teacher has (gave-given) us three tests so far this term.
9. Peter (ridden-rode) his bike to school yesterday.
10. I (took-taken) a shower this morning.
11. Carla and Linda have (grew-grown) two inches in the past year.
12. We have already (took-taken) two courses in American history.

B. Choose between the past tense and the present perfect tense of the verb in front of each sentence. Look at the three examples. Use them as models for your answers.

Examples: (see) I _saw_ the late news last night on television.

(see) I _have seen_ the late news every night this month.

(see) I _have already seen_ the news twice today.

1. (write) Bob _____ to his family three times since he came here.
2. (write) Tom _____ to his girlfriend two days ago.
3. (drive) Mr. Ross _____ to New York yesterday.
4. (drive) My sister _____ to New York twice.
5. (break) My mother _____ several dishes in the past six months.
6. (break) The saucer _____ when I was drying it.
7. (take) The two boys _____ the bus to school yesterday.
8. (take) I _____ that course already.
9. (study) Allison _____ for her math test last night.
10. (study) I _____ that lesson; I don't have to read it again.

Skill Sharpeners 3—Unit 10

Here To Stay (1)

A. Read the story quickly to get a general idea of the subject. Then look at the Vocabulary Highlights. These words are underlined in the story. Be sure you understand the meaning of each word as it is used in the story. Check in the dictionary if you are unsure. Remember, some words have more than one meaning. Write down the meanings of the words that are new to you.

Vocabulary Highlights

| settled | continent | established | failed |
| descendants | actually | disappeared | rough |

B. Now read the story again. Use the dictionary if there are other words you do not understand.

The East Coast

About 35,000 years ago, some Asian hunters walked across Alaska and settled in what is now the United States. At that time, Asia and Alaska were connected by land. The Indians or Native Americans are the descendants of these Asian hunters. As far as anyone knows they were the first people to live in North America. For thousands of years the Indians were the only people to live on the continent, although people from Norway may have visited it in the 11th century. In 1492, things changed. On October 12th of that year, Christopher Columbus discovered "the new world." Within a few years of his discovery, thousands of Europeans sailed across the Atlantic Ocean to explore the new world. Many of these explorers settled in North America.

The Spanish were the first Europeans to actually live in North America. In 1565, Pedro Menendez de Aviles and his men established the first North American city. They called it Saint Augustine. This city still stands today. It is famous for being the oldest city in the United States. Many people go to Florida to visit Saint Augustine every year.

The English were the next group of Europeans to live in North America. In 1584, Sir Walter Raleigh established a settlement on Roanoke Island off the coast of what is now North Carolina. He was the leader of a hundred men and women. It was on this island that Virginia Dare was born. She was the first English child born in the new world. Unfortunately, Virginia Dare and the other citizens of Roanoke Island disappeared one day. No one knows exactly what happened to these people. It is one of the great mysteries of early North American history.

The first successful English settlement in North America was Jamestown in Virginia. Captain John Smith was the leader of the Jamestown settlement. Jamestown almost failed too, but Pocahontas, an Indian woman, saved the life of Captain Smith and convinced the Indians to make peace with the English settlers. After a few difficult years, Jamestown became a rich and lively city.

In 1620, a boat called the *Mayflower* landed about 300 miles north of Jamestown. The people on the boat, the Pilgrims, called their new town Plymouth. They had a difficult time at first, but with the help of friendly Indians, they survived the rough winters and became successful.

After the success of Jamestown and Plymouth, more people decided to move to the new world. At first they settled close to the original settlements, Plymouth and Jamestown. Soon, however, they moved to other parts of the continent. Almost everyone who traveled to North America remained. The early settlers were here to stay.

(Go on to the next page.)

C. **You can often guess what happened from the facts you read. Decide which of the answers best completes the sentence, and circle it.**

The people of Roanoke Island probably

   a. died at the hands of the Indians.
   b. returned to England.
   c. sailed to Saint Augustine.
   d. moved to Jamestown.

D. **Use a word from the Vocabulary Highlights to complete each of these sentences.**

1. James had to repeat Algebra I; he _____ it last term.

2. Asia is the largest _____.

3. The kidnapped children _____ a week ago.

4. My grandparents _____ in Puerto Rico fifty years ago.

5. Things weren't easy for me last year; I had a very _____ time.

E. **Number the statements in the order in which they happened.** The number 1 is done for you.

   _____ Virginia Dare was born.

   _____ The Pilgrims landed at Plymouth.

   __1__ Asians walked across to Alaska and settled in what is now the United States.

   _____ The Spanish established the city of Saint Augustine.

   _____ The British established a settlement on Roanoke Island.

   _____ Captain John Smith led a group of settlers to Jamestown.

   _____ Christopher Columbus sailed across the Atlantic Ocean.

F. **Match the speakers with the quotation that fits best by writing the letter of the quotation in the blank next to the speaker's name.**

1. Christopher Columbus _____
2. Pedro Menendez de Aviles _____
3. Sir Walter Raleigh _____
4. John Smith _____
5. Pocahontas _____

   a. "As the leader of the Jamestown colony, I insist that everyone work hard."

   b. "Men, we have finally reached land! We are the first to discover a new route to a distant land."

   c. "We have to help these strange people, father. They will die without us."

   d. "We will call our new city Saint Augustine."

   e. "The settlers of Roanoke Island are the bravest people to come to the New World."

G. **Use an encyclopedia to find out about some of the other leaders who established settlements on the east coast: New Netherlands, Massachusetts Bay, Rhode Island, Connecticut, Pennsylvania, Maryland, and Georgia. On your paper write a paragraph about one of these settlements and its leader(s).**

Skill Sharpeners 3—Unit 10

Word Skills: Analogies

An analogy is a comparison between two sets of words. To complete an analogy, you must discover the relationship between the words in the first set, and then find a word that makes that same relationship with the first word in the other set. When you are completing the analogies on this page, think about the word skills you have already practiced in this book: synonyms, antonyms, homophones, and categories. These are some of the ways in which words in an analogy can relate to each other. Look at the example below. Choose one of the four answers.

big : little : : old : _____

small   tall   young   quiet

The correct answer is *young*. *Big* and *little* are antonyms, so you must find an antonym for *old*; the only one given is *young*.

(NOTE: You read the analogy as "Big is to little as old is to young.")

Now complete each of the following analogies. Circle your answers.

1. breakfast : morning : : lunch : _____ meal   afternoon   dinner   eat
2. banana : yellow : : apple : _____ food   fruit   fresh   red
3. mouse : mice : : tooth : _____ mouth   white   animal   teeth
4. wall : clock : : wrist : _____ time   arm   watch   o'clock
5. to : too : : write : _____ wrote   paper   right   wrong
6. bottom : top : : cellar : _____ attic   basement   house   down
7. doctor : hospital : : professor : _____ subject   university   teacher   lawyer
8. blood : red : : sugar : _____ sweet   color   salt   white
9. up : down : : in : _____ into   on   out   from
10. glove : hand : : sock : _____ shoe   foot   leg   punch
11. winter : cold : : summer : _____ hot   season   sun   fever
12. ring : finger : : bracelet : _____ jewelry   arm   neck   chest
13. oak : tree : : rose : _____ woman   red   pink   flower
14. chauffeur : car : : pilot : _____ airplane   airport   fly   runway
15. fight : fought : : shoot : _____ gun   shot   enemy   west
16. bad : awful : : good : _____ better   wonderful   terrible   best
17. chemistry : science : : geometry : _____ mathematics   algebra   subject   Greek
18. film : movie : : cheap : _____ costly   store   sale   inexpensive

Two Careers

Look at the chart below. It gives you information about the careers of two people. **Use this information to answer the questions.**

Name	Place of Birth	Date of Birth	Came to U.S.A.	Address in U.S.A	Degrees	College	Occupation Now
Amin Jabbour	Beirut, Lebanon	5/14/50	1/5/71	Quincy, MA 1971–1974 Boston, MA 1974–1976 Austin, TX 1976–	B.S. 1974 (civil engineering) M.S. 1976 (civil engineering)	Northeastern University Mass. Inst. of Technology (MIT)	Professor of Civil Engineering at the University of Texas 1976–
Isabel Minton	Leeds, England	5/3/45			B.A. 1967 (psychology) M.A. 1971 (psychology) Ph.D. 1974 (psychology)	Univ. of Manchester University of London University of London	Psychologist in Bristol, England 1974–

Answer the questions on your paper. Use complete sentences.

Professor Jabbour

1. Where was Professor Jabbour born?
2. When was he born?
3. Has he ever been to the U.S.A.?
4. When did he come to the U.S.A.?
5. Where did he live when he first came to the United States?
6. Where else has he lived?
7. How many times has he moved?
8. Where is he living now?
9. How long has he lived there?
10. How many degrees has he earned?
11. When did he get his B.S.? His M.S.?
12. After he got his B.S., how long did it take him to get his M.S.?
13. How many colleges has he attended?
14. What was his major field in college?
15. What is his occupation now?
16. How long has he been in the U.S.A.?
17. How old is he?

Dr. Minton

1. Where was Dr. Minton born?
2. When was she born?
3. How old is she?
4. Has she ever been to the U.S.A.?
5. How many degrees has she earned?
6. When did she get her B.A.? Her M.A.? Her Ph.D.?
7. What was her major field at the University of Manchester?
8. How many different universities has she attended?
9. How many years did it take her to get her Ph.D. after her M.A.?
10. What is her occupation now?
11. Where does she work?
12. How long has she been working in her present occupation?
13. How old was she when she graduated from the University of Manchester?

NOTE: MA is the standard post office abbreviation for Massachusetts.
TX is the standard post office abbreviation for Texas.

Skill Objectives: Interpreting a chart, reviewing verb tenses
Examine the chart as a class. If needed, explain the abbreviated dates and the meaning and pronunciation of the degree titles. Adjust the amount of preliminary discussion to the needs of your class, then assign the page as independent work. **Extension Activities:** 1) Have the class discuss ways in which Amin Jabbour and Isabel Minton are alike, and ways in which they are different. 2) Have students write a short biography of Amin or Isabel based on the information in the chart.

Skill Sharpeners 3—Unit 10

Dear Dot

Dear Dot—

My girlfriend Karen has broken several dates with me recently. She calls me on the day of our date and says that she can't make it. Sometimes she explains, but most times she doesn't. Last week I drove to her apartment and I found a note on her door. It said that she was at her sister's house. I called the number she put in the note, but there was no answer. I have talked to Karen about this situation. She says that she still loves me, and that if I am patient, everything is going to be all right. I am trying to be patient, but I am getting tired of her canceling our dates. What's your opinion, Dot? What should I do?

Ted

1. What has happened to Ted recently? _____

2. Does Karen explain when she breaks a date? _____

3. What happened last week? _____

4. Where did Karen say she was going to be? _____

5. What is Ted getting tired of? _____

6. What does the word *canceling* mean in this letter? Circle the best answer.

   a. calling about   b. calling for   c. calling off   d. calling in

7. What is your advice to Ted? Discuss your answer in class. Then read Dot's answer and tell why you agree or disagree. Dot's advice is below.

Dear Ted—

Try not calling or making dates for a couple of weeks. Karen might be trying to tell you that she isn't interested anymore, but she might also be having problems, perhaps with someone in her family. If you really love her, give her the time she asks for. If you aren't serious about each other, however, this might be a good time to get out of this relationship.

Dot

Write About It

Pretend you are Karen. On your paper, write a letter to Ted explaining what you have been doing for the last six weeks and why you haven't been able to see him.

Skill Sharpeners 3—Unit 10

Word Skills: Irregular Verbs

A. Many of the verbs we use most often in English are irregular in the simple past tense. **Write the simple past form of each of the following verbs. Use the dictionary if you need to.** The first one is done for you.

begin	*began*	fly	_____	ring	_____
bite	_____	get	_____	run	_____
blow	_____	give	_____	say	_____
break	_____	go	_____	see	_____
bring	_____	grow	_____	sell	_____
build	_____	have	_____	send	_____
buy	_____	hear	_____	shoot	_____
catch	_____	hit	_____	sing	_____
choose	_____	hold	_____	sit	_____
come	_____	keep	_____	sleep	_____
cost	_____	know	_____	speak	_____
cut	_____	lead	_____	stand	_____
do	_____	leave	_____	steal	_____
drink	_____	lose	_____	swim	_____
drive	_____	make	_____	take	_____
eat	_____	meet	_____	teach	_____
fall	_____	pay	_____	tell	_____
feel	_____	put	_____	think	_____
fight	_____	read	_____	win	_____
find	_____	ride	_____	write	_____

B. From the list above, choose 25 of the verbs you know well. On your paper, write a sentence for each one, using the simple past tense. For example, *We began class early yesterday.*

Skill Sharpeners 3—Unit 11

Crossword Puzzle

Write the words in the right places. Number 1 Across and number 1 Down are done for you.

Across

1. what they did at the beach
4. battled
6. operated the car
7. what they did with the milk
10. kept out of sight
11. looked at or watched
12. I _____, I saw, I conquered.
13. didn't win
15. what the wind did
17. discovered
19. what the thief did
20. what the bicyclist did
21. mailed the letter
22. received
23. listened
26. constructed
28. said

Down

1. what the singers did
2. she _____ her bed
3. smashed the glass
4. what the pilot did
5. same as 23 across
8. was aware of
9. donated
10. She _____ the baby in her arms.
12. selected
14. wondered
15. She _____ home the bacon.
16. He _____ his new suit.
18. didn't give away
19. didn't stand
24. what the diners did
25. He _____ his homework.
26. what the mad dog did
27. what the front person did

(Answers on page 125)

By Myself

A. Complete each sentence with one of the following *reflexive pronouns*:

myself   yourself   himself   herself   itself   ourselves   yourselves   themselves

1. I like _____.
2. The baby can dress _____.
3. The young man is painting a picture of _____.
4. We are buying _____ new coats today.
5. Lina is recording _____ on the tape recorder.
6. You students can be proud of _____.
7. The women built the houses _____.
8. It's true; I read it _____ last week.
9. No one is helping Paul; he's painting the fence _____.
10. You have to ask _____, "Is this the right thing to do?"
11. The firemen can't control the fire; it's going to burn _____ out.
12. Please help _____ to more food, Donna.
13. The girls are going to the library to find the answers _____.
14. We want the house for _____ this weekend.
15. He always looks at _____ in the mirror before he leaves home.

B. Complete each sentence with the correct subject pronoun (I, you, he, she, it, we, they).

1. _____ can see myself in these dishes.
2. _____ hit himself in the head.
3. _____ call ourselves bilingual.
4. _____ dresses herself in red every day.
5. _____ stopped yourself just in time.
6. _____ blame myself for losing the money.
7. _____ have to read this yourself.
8. _____ is always talking to himself.
9. _____ need the money themselves.

Skill Sharpeners 3—Unit 11

Water, Water Everywhere

Water is everywhere. More than three-fourths of the surface of the earth is covered by water. Everything that lives depends on water. People can get along without food for long periods, but they cannot live without water. We drink water, we swim in it, we travel on it, wash our clothes in it, and cook in it. And of course, all the fish we eat comes from the water.

Where does our water come from? Where does it go? Water is made up of two gases that we find in nature, hydrogen and oxygen. But most of the water on the earth has been here for millions of years. The water that falls as rain on your roof is the same water that fell as rain thousands of years ago. The water moves in a cycle. Let's follow a drop. As you read about the cycle, look at the picture. Use your dictionary if there are words you don't know.

1. A drop of water is on the surface of the ocean. Sunlight warms the water.
2. The drop of water evaporates and turns into water vapor—tiny droplets that float in the air.
3. The water vapor from many drops joins together to form a cloud.
4. Wind blows the cloud. When the cloud meets cold air, it turns back into drops of water and falls as rain.
5. The rain falls on land and helps plants grow. Some of it falls on mountains and flows back to the ocean as streams and rivers.
6. Some water soaks into the soil and moves underground. It comes back up to the surface through springs and wells.

After it is used, it flows back into the soil or into rivers and then into the ocean.

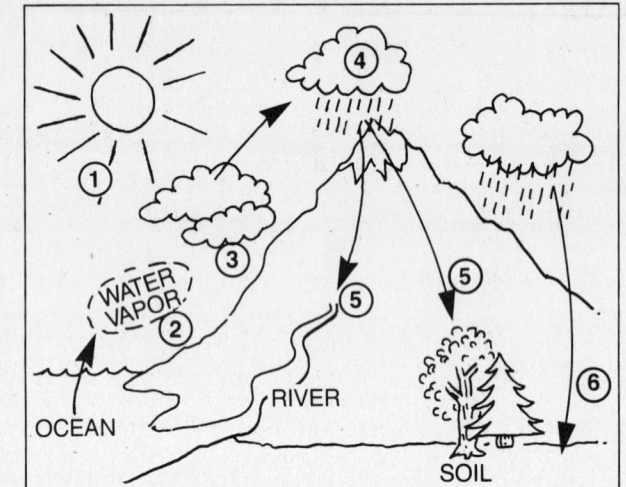

A. **Look at the diagram of the water cycle below. Fill in the blanks to complete the diagram.** The numbers refer to the description of the cycle above.

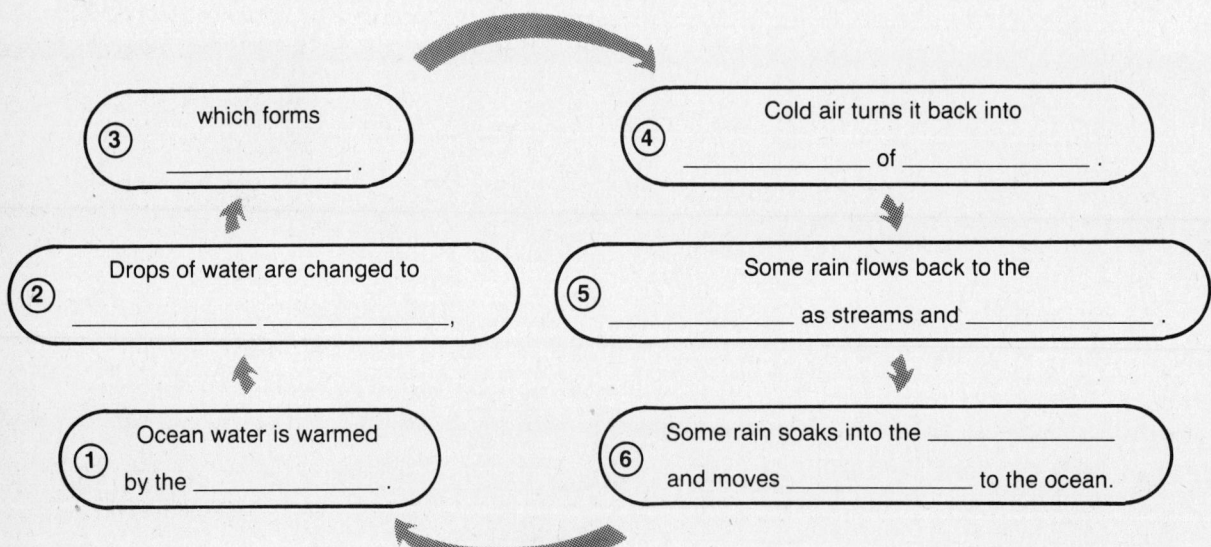

③ which forms _____.

④ Cold air turns it back into _____ of _____.

② Drops of water are changed to _____,

⑤ Some rain flows back to the _____ as streams and _____.

① Ocean water is warmed by the _____.

⑥ Some rain soaks into the _____ and moves _____ to the ocean.

B. **On your paper, write about your feelings about water. Do you live near the ocean or a large lake? Would you like to? Why or why not? Have you had important experiences connected with water? What were they?**

Television Tonight

Here is part of the television program for one evening in a large city area. **Use the program to answer the questions.** The first one is done for you.

6:00
- ☐ Sesame Street (CC) 2
- ☐ News 4-5-6-7-9-10-12
- ☐ Oceanus 11
- ☐ CHiPs Patrol 25
- ☐ Nashville Music 27
- ☐ 3-2-1 Contact (R) (CC) . . 36
- ☐ M*A*S*H 38
- ☐ Personal Finance 44
- ☐ Happy Days Again 56

6:30
- ☐ CBS News 6
- ☐ ABC News (CC) 9-12
- ☐ NBC News 10
- ☐ Doctor Who 11
- ☐ News 27
- ☐ Business Report . . . 36-44
- ☐ The Jeffersons 38
- ☐ Laverne & Shirley 56

7:00
- ☐ Doctor Who 2
- ☐ NBC News 4
- ☐ ABC News (CC) 5
- ☐ The Muppets 6-9
- ☐ CBS News 7
- ☐ P.M. Magazine 10
- ☐ Business Report 11
- ☐ Tic Tac Dough 12
- ☐ State House Report . . . 36
- ☐ M*A*S*H 38
- ☐ Business of Management 44
- ☐ Three's Company 56

7:30
- ☐ Wild, Wild World of Animals 2
- ☐ Evening Magazine / Amazing kid composer; a man who buys and sells through the classified ads 4
- ☐ Chronicle 5
- ☐ You Asked For It 6
- ☐ Entertainment Tonight . 7-10
- ☐ People's Court 9
- ☐ MacNeil/Lehrer . . 11-36-44
- ☐ Family Feud 12
- ☐ WKRP In Cincinnati . . . 25
- ☐ Barney Miller 38
- ☐ Three's Company 56

8:00
- ☐ Nova / A new theory as to why the dinosaurs died out after 150 million years of successful dominance. (R) (CC) 2-11
- ☐ The A-Team / The A-Team is hired to locate a kidnaped mathematician 4-10
- ☐ Happy Days / A former Falcon asks Fonzie to be the best man at his wedding. (CC) . . 5-9
- ☐ Movie / "Will There Really Be a Morning?" (Premiere) Susan Blakely, Lee Grant . 6-7
- ☐ Movie / "Dr Jekyll and Mr. Hyde" (1941) Spencer Tracy, Ingrid Bergman 25
- ☐ Ireland: A TV History . . 36
- ☐ Movie / "Cinderella Liberty" (1973) James Caan, Marsha Mason 38
- ☐ Organizational Planning and Implementation 44
- ☐ Movie / "Brannigan" (1975) John Wayne, Richard Attenborough 56

8:30
- ☐ Laverne & Shirley / Lenny and Squiggy set off on a frantic search when they find a treasure map. (CC) 5-9
- ☐ America: The Second Century 44

9:00
- ☐ American Playhouse / "The File On Jill Hatch: 1950s–early 1970s" Carl accepts a teaching position at Roosevelt University in Chicago; Sheila gets involved in the civil rights movement after their child, Jill, is born. (Part 2) (CC) 2-11-36
- ☐ Bare Essence / When Tyger sets out to expand the perfume line into a cosmetics business she discovers that Hadden's conglomerate is on shaky financial ground 4-10
- ☐ Three's Company / Jack is forced into a bout with a professional boxer after defending Furley at the Regal Beagle. (CC) 5-9
- ☐ Making It Count 44

9:30
- ☐ 9 To 5 / Violet's romance with a young executive leads to the offer of a big promotion for her 5-9
- ☐ Religious Quest 44

10:00
- ☐ News 2
- ☐ St. Elsewhere / Dr. Auschlander must decide whether to undergo chemotherapy; a female flasher prowls the halls of St. Eligius. (Part 1) . . . 4-10
- ☐ Hart To Hart / While at a gala weekend event, Jonathan and Jennifer discover a wealthy recluse is being impersonated by his aides. (CC) 5-9-12
- ☐ Frederick Douglass, Slave and Statesman / Actor William Marshall portrays the great black leader 11
- ☐ Frontline / What would happen if the U.S. budgets unprecedented amounts for defense spending during an economic recession. (CC) 44
- ☐ CNN News 56

CC = closed captioned for people with hearing problems
R = repeat program

1. You can watch the news at 6:00 on channels <u>4</u> <u>5</u> <u>6</u> <u>7</u> <u>9</u> <u>10</u> <u>12</u>

2. The schedule gives programs starting at _____.

3. The movie "Dr. Jekyll and Mr. Hyde" was made in the year _____.

4. "Hart To Hart" is on channels _____, _____, and _____.

5. How many movies are being shown on TV tonight? _____

6. If you want to see a TV program with Lenny and Squiggy, turn to channel _____ at _____ P.M. The name of the program is _____.

7. People with hearing problems can watch close captioned news on channels ____ and ____ at ____ P.M. and on channel ____ at ____ P.M.

8. The stars of "Cinderella Liberty" are _____ and _____.

9. The "Nova" program at 8:00 is about _____.

10. Is this the first time this "Nova" program has been shown? _____

11. "Three's Company" is on channel ____ at ____ P.M. and on channel ____ at ____ P.M.

Skill Objective: Reading a TV schedule
Have students skim the TV guide. Ask various students, *What show would you watch at 8:00? What channel is it on? When is the show over?* Assign the page for independent work. Extension Activities: Ask students to get a TV schedule for the coming week, and each day, circle the shows they watch. Encourage discussions about favorite shows. At the end of the week, have students graph the number of hours they watched TV each day. Bar or line graphs can be used.

Skill Sharpeners 3—Unit 11   105

Here To Stay (2)

A. Read the story quickly to get a general idea of the subject. Then look at the Vocabulary Highlights. These words are underlined in the story. Be sure you understand the meaning of each word as it is used in the story. Check in the dictionary if you are unsure. Remember, some words have more than one meaning. Write down the meanings of the words that are new to you.

Vocabulary Highlights

led	priests
briefly	mission
admiral	provided
buccaneer	crowds
claimed	fortune

B. Now read the story again. Use the dictionary if there are other words you do not understand.

The West Coast

Juan Cabrillo Rodriguez was the first European to explore California. In 1542, he led a group of Spanish sailors from Mexico up the Pacific coast of North America. They explored about 75 miles of the California coast. They stopped briefly at present-day San Diego, but they did not settle in California. The sailors returned to Mexico.

The next important visitor to California was the English admiral and buccaneer, Sir Francis Drake. In 1579, Drake landed on the California coast and explored the land near what is now San Francisco. Drake claimed the entire northwest coast of North America for England. Neither he nor his men stayed to live on the land. They left North America to the Indians who were already living there.

It wasn't until 1769 that the first Europeans began to live in California. Father Junipero Serra and other Spanish priests started the first mission in San Diego in that year. After the Mexican Revolution in 1823, California oficially became part of Mexico. By 1846, there were 21 missions along the coast of California. The missions stretched from San Diego to San Francisco. They provided training and education for the Indians. By 1846, however, large ranch owners took over the missions.

In that year, Mexico and the United States went to war. At the end of the war, California became a part of the United States. The priests returned to Mexico, and American settlers moved into California.

In 1848, a man named James Marshall found gold at John Sutter's mill, near present-day Sacramento. At first, no one paid attention to the discovery, but by 1849, crowds of people were coming to find their fortunes. In the four years after the discovery of gold, the population of California grew from 15,000 to 250,000! Soon, settlers were moving north to what today we call the states of Oregon and Washington. The new settlers came from the East to live on this land. They worked hard to build new lives for themselves. They didn't want to go back East. Like the first settlers of Plymouth and Jamestown, they were here to stay.

(Go on to the next page.)

C. **What is this story mostly about? Circle your answer.**
   a. the discovery of gold in California
   b. the California coast
   c. the early history of California
   d. the American Indians in California

D. **Use a word from the Vocabulary Highlights to complete each of these sentences.**
   1. Mr. Chin won a _____ in the lottery last week.
   2. There were _____ of people at the airport to see the stars.
   3. Janet was in a hurry, so we spoke only _____.
   4. There were several _____ at the church last week.
   5. The general _____ his troops into battle and won.

E. **Number the statements in the order in which they happened in the story.** The number 1 is done for you.

   _____ California became a part of the United States.
   _1_ Juan Cabrillo Rodriguez led Spanish sailors up the coast of California.
   _____ Father Junipero Serra began the California missions.
   _____ Drake claimed all of the Northwest for England.
   _____ California became part of Mexico.
   _____ The Mexican-American war began.
   _____ Sir Francis Drake landed in California.
   _____ People came west to look for gold.
   _____ James Marshall found gold at Sutter's mill.

F. **Draw a line from each quotation at the left to the name of the most likely speaker.**

   1. "The Indians need our help. We can teach them our language, our religion, and our culture at the missions."
   2. "Gold! I've found gold!"
   3. "There are people all over my property looking for gold."
   4. "I claim this land for Her Majesty Queen Elizabeth."
   5. "Back to the ships, men, and we sail back south. We've seen all there is to see here."

   a. Juan Cabrillo Rodriguez
   b. Sir Francis Drake
   c. Father Junipero Serra
   d. John Sutter
   e. James Marshall

Skill Sharpeners 3—Unit 11

Two Couples

A. Read the story. Then answer the questions. Use complete sentences. The first one is done for you.

Hop Nguyen came to Canton, Ohio, from Vietnam with her husband, Vuong, in 1978. When they first came, Vuong found a job in a Chinese restaurant. He worked there for only one year, because he found a better job with a computer company, where he still works today. Hop also found a job when she first came. She worked in a day-care center. When she first started there, she was a day-care worker, but now she is the manager. Both Hop and Vuong went to English classes when they first arrived, but now they study English only one night a week at the Adult Education Center.

1. When did Hop and Vuong come to the United States? _They came to the United States in 1978._

2. Where did Vuong work when he first came? _____

3. In what year did he start to work for a computer company? _____

4. How long has he been working at the computer company? _____

5. When did Hop first find a job? _____

6. Is she working for the day-care center now? _____

7. How long has she been working there? _____

8. When did Hop and Vuong begin to study English? _____

9. How long have they been studying English? _____

10. How long have they been in the United States? _____

B. Read the story about Jose and Daysi. On your paper, write questions like the ones about Hop and Vuong. Then write answers to the questions. You may wish to exchange papers with a partner and answer each other's questions.

Jose Rodriguez came to Dallas in 1970. He started to work at the bank at that time. A year later he bought a car, and in 1972 he was married to Daysi Ayala. In 1974, Jose and Daysi bought a house, and in 1975, their first child, Maria Elena, was born.

Today, Jose and Daysi still live in Dallas. Jose still works at the same bank, still drives the same car, and still lives in the same house. But today Jose and Daysi have three children.

Dear Dot

Dear Dot—

My husband Jack is teaching our daughters to work with tools and fix things around the house—even the car. He says that nowadays girls have to be able to do things for themselves. I don't know how to fix the car or a sink or anything, for that matter, and to tell the truth, I really don't want to know. The girls seem to like doing the work, but I'm not sure if it is such a good idea. The other day I found them in the attic, trying to fix an old television set. I'm afraid that they could hurt themselves. What do you think? Should I put a stop to all this?

Old-Fashioned Mother

1. What is Jack doing for his daughters? _____

2. Why is he doing this? _____

3. How do the girls feel about their lessons? _____

4. What is Old-Fashioned Mother afraid of? _____

5. What does the word *seem* mean in this letter? Circle your answer.

   a. appear   b. need   c. looked   d. want

6. What is your advice to Old-Fashioned Mother? Discuss your answer in class. Then read Dot's answer. Tell why you agree or disagree. Dot's advice is below.

Dear Old-Fashioned—

Not at all. Your girls are lucky indeed to have a father who teaches them these skills. They are going to need to know about these things. You probably wouldn't worry about your sons fixing machines and cars. Your daughters are just as capable. Leave them alone. You may be glad they have this knowledge if something goes wrong some day when your husband is away!

Dot

Write About It

Think of something you know how to do well—make scrambled eggs, change a tire, paint a room, build a camp fire, or anything else—and write clear directions for doing that activity. Write as if you were writing directions for someone who has never done this activity before.

Skill Sharpeners 3—Unit 11

Skill Objectives: Reading for details, understanding words through context, making judgments, writing directions. Have students read the letter and answer the questions independently. Students can write their advice to "Old-Fashioned Mother" on a separate sheet of paper. Correct the first five questions as a class, then have students compare and discuss their own advice and Dot's reply. You may wish to assign the "Write About It" topic as homework.

Word Skills: Adding "er" and "est"

When you compare two things, you use the ending *er*. For example, **Juan is shorter than Jose.** When you compare three or more things, you use the ending *est*. For example, **Ronnie is the shortest boy on the team.** Here are some rules to help you add these endings.

Rule 1: For words that end in *e*, drop the *e* and add *er* or *est*. Examples: *large, larger, largest; free, freer, freest.*

Rule 2: For words that end in a consonant followed by *y*, change the *y* to *i* and add *er* or *est*. Example: *pretty, prettier, prettiest.*

Rule 3: For one-syllable words that end in consonant-vowel-consonant, double the last consonant and add *er* or *est*. Example: *sad, sadder, saddest.*

NOTE: The words *good* and *bad* never take *er* or *est*. They have special forms. We say *good, better, best; bad, worse, worst.*

A. Add *er* and *est* to the following words. Use the rules to help you. The first one is done for you.

	word	er	est
1.	big	bigger	biggest
2.	cool		
3.	funny		
4.	great		
5.	long		
6.	young		
7.	dry		
8.	wet		
9.	lazy		
10.	hot		
11.	angry		
12.	chubby		
13.	sunny		
14.	thin		
15.	little		
16.	warm		
17.	tiny		
18.	fat		
19.	blue		
20.	red		

B. Adjectives with *er* are called *comparative*. Adjectives with *est* are called *superlative*. **Now write a sentence using each of the comparatives and superlatives you made above. Include also sentences for the comparative and superlative of *good* and *bad*.**

110   Skill Sharpeners 3—Unit 12

Pat, June, and Alice

A. Look at the illustrations. Then answer the questions. The first two are done for you.

1. Who is the oldest? _____
   Pat is the oldest.

2. Who is older, June or Alice? _____
   June is older than Alice.

3. Who is older, Pat or June? _____

4. Who is the youngest? _____

5. Who is younger, Alice or June? _____

6. Who is the tallest? _____

7. Who is the shortest? _____

8. Who is taller, June or Pat? _____

9. Who is shorter, June or Alice? _____

10. Who is the strongest? _____

11. Who is stronger, Dick or Sid? _____

12. Is Sol stronger than Dick? _____

13. Who is the thinnest? _____

14. Who is thinner, Tom or George? _____

15. Who is the chubbiest? _____

16. Who is chubbier, Ed or George? _____

B. Pierre has three girlfriends. He likes them all, but Lisa is his favorite. **Tell about them.** The first line is done for you.

	Anne	Gina	Lisa
kind	*Anne is kind.*	*Gina is kinder than Anne.*	*Lisa is the kindest.*
smart			
friendly			
nice			

Skill Objective: Constructing comparatives and superlatives
Assign this page as independent work. Correct as a class.

Skill Sharpeners 3—Unit 12

Vacation Time

Travel is big business. Hotels, airlines, and travel agents advertise in newspapers and magazines to attract visitors to vacation spots. Here are three advertisements. **Complete them with appropriate words.** The first one is done for you. **Use comparatives in the second advertisement and superlatives in the third.**

COME TO BEAUTIFUL BERMUDA!
The beaches are _clean_ and _white_!
The weather is _warm_ and _sunny_!
The people are _friendly_!
The hotels are _grand_!
The food is _tasty_!
The rooms are _large_ and _lovely_!
Yes, come to Bermuda, and you'll have a _great_ time!
ONLY $399!
HOTEL & AIR FARE

COME TO ROMANTIC ARUBA!
The beaches are _cleaner_ and _whiter_!
The weather is _____ and _____!
The people are _____!
The hotels are _____!
The food is _____!
The rooms are _____ and _____!
Yes, come to Aruba, and you'll have a _____ time!
ONLY $299!
HOTEL & AIR FARE

COME TO SUPER ST. THOMAS!
The beaches are _the cleanest_ and _whitest_!
The weather is _____ and _____!
The people are _____!
The hotels are _____!
The food is _____!
The rooms are _____ and _____!
Yes, come to St. Thomas and you'll have _____ time!
ONLY $199!
HOTEL & AIR FARE

Skill Objective: Using comparatives and superlatives
Review the directions with the class, then assign this page as independent work.

More Vacation Time

Words with more than two syllables usually do not use *er* and *est* to form the comparative and superlative. Instead, they use the words *more* and *the most*. The comparative of *exciting* is *more exciting*. The superlative is *the most exciting*. Use this rule in helping you write advertisements for these three ski vacation sports. Use comparatives and superlatives in your ads.

Skill Objectives: Constructing comparatives and superlatives using *more* and *the most*.

Write the first travel ad as a class, using the information in the ad and following the style set on page 112: *The mountains are high. The snow is beautiful. . . . The lift tickets are cheap.* etc. You may wish to have the class compose the other two ads orally before assigning the page as independent work. Extension Activity: Have students write a travel ad, using superlatives to describe their school, town, favorite store or native country.

$399.00
HOTEL & AIR
ONE WEEK!

High mountains
Beautiful snow
Cool, clear days
Lift tickets
$15/day
Good discos
Interesting people

$350.00
HOTEL & AIR
ONE WEEK!

High mountains
Beautiful snow
Cool, clear days
Lift tickets
$12/day
Good discos
Interesting people

$299.00
HOTEL & AIR
ONE WEEK!

High mountains
Beautiful snow
Cool, clear days
Lift tickets
$10/day
Good discos
Interesting people

COME TO THE MOUNTAINS
OF MONTANA!

_____
_____
_____
_____
_____
_____
_____
_____
_____
_____

COME TO THE WHITE MOUNTAINS
OF NEW HAMPSHIRE!

_____
_____
_____
_____
_____
_____
_____
_____
_____
_____

COME TO THE COLORADO ROCKIES!

_____
_____
_____
_____
_____
_____
_____
_____
_____
_____

Skill Sharpeners 3—Unit 12

Inflation

Inflation refers to the rate at which the cost of living goes up. An inflation rate of 10% means that something that cost a dollar a year ago costs $1.10 now. The graph shows the rate of inflation, month by month, in 1982 and part of 1983. The numbers at the left of the graph are the annual (whole year) rate of inflation.

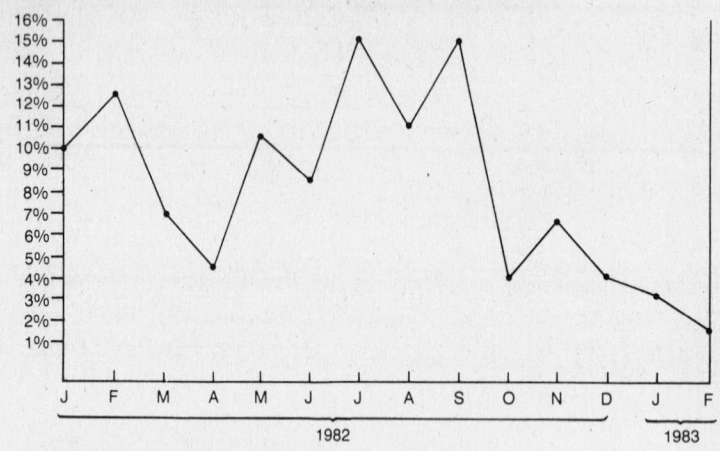

A. Look at the graph. Then use it to answer the questions.

1. What two months had the highest rate of inflation? _____

2. What month had the lowest rate of inflation? _____

3. Was inflation higher in January of 1982 or January of 1983? _____

4. When did inflation rise the most? From what month to what month? _____

5. When did it fall most sharply? _____

6. During which months was inflation higher than 8%? _____

7. During which months was inflation lower than 8%? _____

8. About what was the inflation rate in March of 1982? _____

9. About what was the inflation rate in November of 1982? _____

10. When was the inflation rate higher, in the summer or the winter of 1982? _____

B. This kind of graph is called a line graph. **Make a line graph to show the temperature, hour by hour, one spring day. Use the following information:**

8:00 AM 55°F	11:00 AM 72°F	2:00 PM 82°F	5:00 PM 80°F	8:00 PM 70°F
9:00 AM 62°F	12:00 noon 75°F	3:00 PM 85°F	6:00 PM 76°F	9:00 PM 64°F
10:00 AM 68°F	1:00 PM 78°F	4:00 PM 83°F	7:00 PM 72°F	10:00 PM 59°F

Skill Sharpeners 3—Unit 12

Summer Jobs

Look at these advertisements for summer jobs. Use them to answer the questions.

> **YARD WORK**
> Mon, Wed, Fri afternoons. $3.15/hr. to start. Mowing, gardening, gen. maintenance. Call 332-0066 for appt.

> **MONTANO'S BAKERY**
> Baker's Assistant needed 6 days, 6 AM–12 noon. Apply 27 Chestnut St., Bixford. No phone calls, please.

> **SUMMER ONLY—BUS BOYS**
> at Chef's Delight. No experience necessary. Openings in Bixford and Yorktown. 5–10 PM.

> **MOTHER'S HELPER NEEDED**
> For 2 small children, Mon–Fri, 9 to 12 noon. Some light housework. References required. Call for appointment 498-7531, between 2 and 5.

> **GAS STATION ATTENDANT**
> Gas & oil only. Prefer some experience but will train right person. 10 AM–5 PM. Good pay. Apply in person. MUTUAL OIL COMPANY, 194 Whiting St., Bixford.

> **CASHIER**
> Carl's Coffee Shop, 7AM–2PM, June 25 to Sept. 1 only. No experience necessary. Apply in person, 33 Main St., Rockland.

1. For summer employment, many managers ask that you apply in person. Which jobs here request that you apply in person?
   _____
   _____

2. Only one of the job listings tells you the salary. Which one is it?
   _____
   _____

3. Which job listings say they will take a person with no experience?
   _____
   _____

4. Name two jobs that are mornings only.
   _____
   _____

5. Name one summer job that is evenings only.
   _____

6. Some summer jobs are part-time (about 20 hours a week). How many of these jobs are part time? What are they?
   _____
   _____
   _____

7. Does the gas station attendant have to fix cars?
   _____

8. Will the mother's helper probably have to wash some dishes and vacuum some rugs? Answer yes or no.
   _____

MEMORY BANK

| experience | apply | train | employment |
| employer | part-time | salary | |

Skill Sharpeners 3—Unit 12

Fact or Opinion?

You remember that a fact is a generally accepted statement of truth that can be checked in a dictionary, encyclopedia, or other reference book. An opinion, on the other hand, expresses a personal feeling, idea, or point of view.

Read the following statements. Decide if each is a fact or an opinion. If it is a fact, circle the F; if it is an opinion, circle the O.

F O 1. The United States is larger than Cuba.
F O 2. Summer is the best season of the year.
F O 3. California is prettier than New York.
F O 4. St. Augustine is the oldest city in the United States.
F O 5. The Rocky Mountains are higher than the Appalachians.
F O 6. Movies are more interesting than television programs.
F O 7. Spanish is more difficult to learn than French.
F O 8. Puppies are the cutest of all baby animals.
F O 9. Alaska is the largest of the fifty states.
F O 10. The Pacific Ocean is the largest of the four oceans.
F O 11. Apples are more delicious than oranges.
F O 12. Fresh fruit is more nutritious than potato chips.
F O 13. The Nile is the longest river in the world.
F O 14. Paris is the most interesting city in Europe.
F O 15. The moon is the earth's closest neighbor in the sky.
F O 16. China has the largest population of any country in the world.
F O 17. Hurricanes occur most often in the summer.
F O 18. George Washington was the best United States President.
F O 19. Cancer is the worst disease that a person can have.
F O 20. Christopher Columbus crossed the ocean in 1492.
F O 21. The atom is a very small particle of matter.
F O 22. The Declaration of Independence is a radical document.
F O 23. Liver is richer in vitamin B than eggs.
F O 24. The sun is farther away from the earth than is Mars.
F O 25. The American colonists were right to revolt against the British.
F O 26. Thomas Edison was the greatest American inventor.
F O 27. Train travel is more comfortable than plane travel.
F O 28. There is no life as we know it on the moon.
F O 29. Democracy is the best form of government.
F O 30. Gold is more expensive than silver.

Skill Objective: Discriminating between fact and opinion. Read the introductory paragraph aloud. Complete and discuss the first few items as a class, then assign the page as independent work.

The Sunshine State

Read the article and look at the map. Then answer the questions about Florida.

Florida is a middle-sized state. It is a peninsula in the southeastern United States, and has the longest ocean coastline of any state. The city of Key West is the southernmost city in the United States. Florida is the second fastest growing state. Only California is growing faster.

Florida is a famous resort state, because the climate is warm in the winter, the beaches are beautiful, and the fishing is excellent. The most popular resort cities on the east coast are Miami Beach and Palm Beach. On the west coast, St. Petersburg and Tampa are popular. St. Augustine, in the northern part of the state, is the oldest city in the United States, founded in 1565.

Orlando is the city where Walt Disney World and the Epcot Center are located. About 40,000 tourists visit Disney World every day. The Orlando airport is a very busy place—almost as busy as Miami's airport, which is one of the busiest in the country. Cape Canaveral, about forty miles east of Orlando, is often in the news because it is a test center for satellites, missiles, the space shuttle, and other United States spaceships.

Many of the people in Florida make their living from the tourist trade, but fruit raising and farming are also important. Oranges, grapefruit, and other citrus fruit grow across central Florida from the Atlantic Ocean to the Gulf of Mexico. Frozen orange juice is one of Florida's most important products.

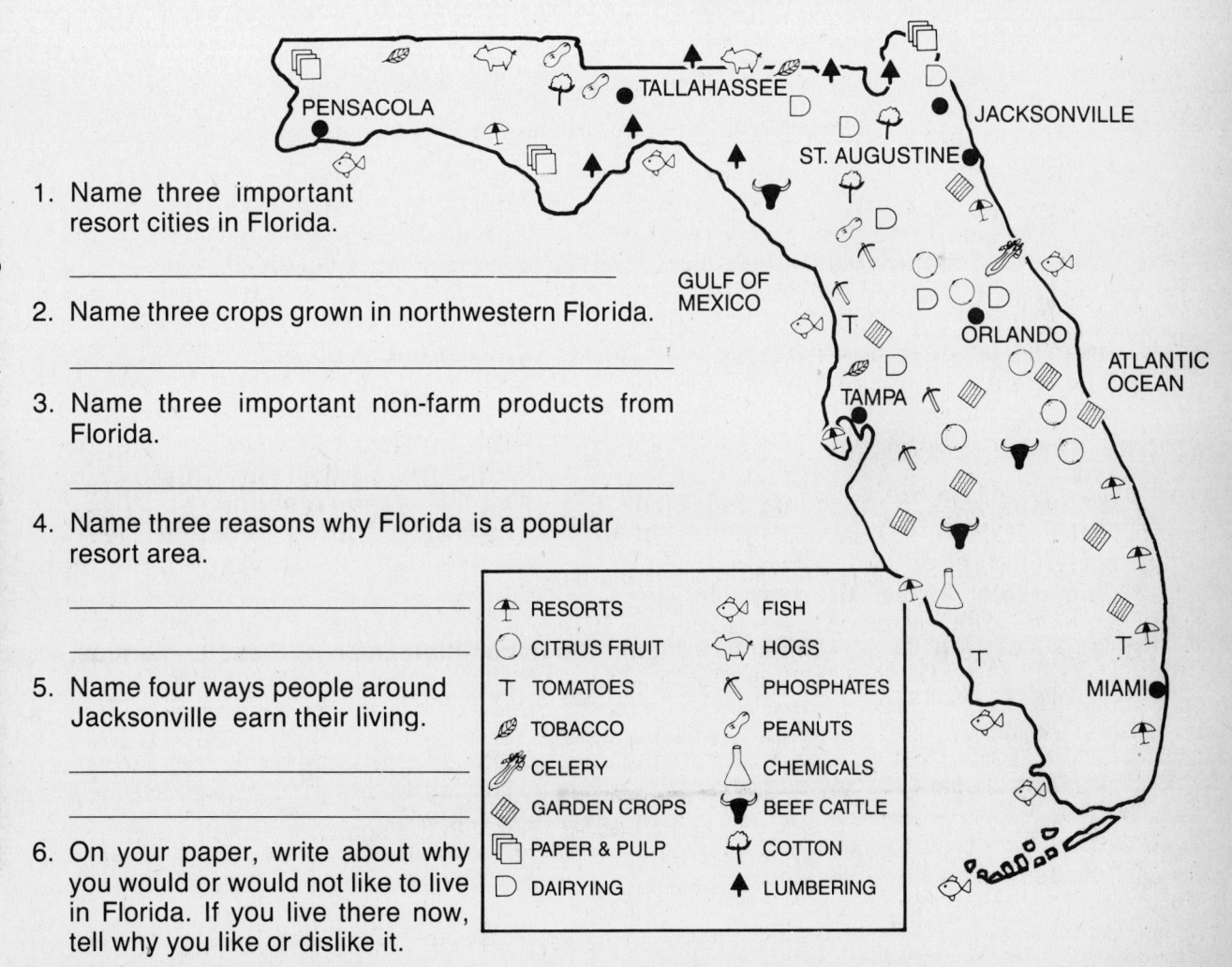

1. Name three important resort cities in Florida.
   _____

2. Name three crops grown in northwestern Florida.
   _____

3. Name three important non-farm products from Florida.
   _____

4. Name three reasons why Florida is a popular resort area.
   _____
   _____

5. Name four ways people around Jacksonville earn their living.
   _____
   _____

6. On your paper, write about why you would or would not like to live in Florida. If you live there now, tell why you like or dislike it.

Map Key:
- ☂ RESORTS
- ○ CITRUS FRUIT
- T TOMATOES
- 🌿 TOBACCO
- CELERY
- GARDEN CROPS
- PAPER & PULP
- D DAIRYING
- 🐟 FISH
- 🐖 HOGS
- PHOSPHATES
- PEANUTS
- CHEMICALS
- BEEF CATTLE
- COTTON
- ▲ LUMBERING

Skill Objectives: Reading for details, interpreting a map with product symbols. Locate Florida on a U.S. map. Have students read the story silently. Discuss unfamiliar words. Have students reread the article, underlining each city or body of water as it is mentioned, and finding that place on the Florida map. Draw attention to the map key. Ask, *Where is lumbering done? What crops are grown around (Orlando)?* Have students answer questions 1-5 individually or in pairs. Question 6 may be assigned as homework.

Skill Sharpeners 3—Unit 12

117

Biggest, Largest, Longest!

A. Read the story quickly to get a general idea of the subject. Then look at the Vocabulary Highlights. These words are underlined in the story. Be sure you understand the meaning of each word as it is used in the story. Check in the dictionary if you are unsure. Remember, some words have more than one meaning. Write down the meanings of the words that are new to you.

Vocabulary Highlights

whale	ostrich
weigh	falcon
ton	cheetah
insect	leopard
tortoise	penny

B. Now read the story again. Use the dictionary if there are other words you do not understand.

Animal Champions

Zoologists, scientists who study animals, tell us the following facts about animals:

- The blue <u>whale</u> is the largest animal in the world. It can be 100 feet long and can <u>weigh</u> more than 100 <u>tons</u>.
- The longest <u>insect</u> is the walking stick. It can be up to 16 inches long.
- The largest fish is the shark. (Remember, a whale is not a fish; it is a mammal.) Sharks can be 45 feet long.
- The giant <u>tortoise</u> of South America has the longest life of any animal. These turtles can live to be 150 years old.
- The <u>ostrich</u> is the largest bird. Ostriches can be 8 feet tall. They can weigh 200 pounds.
- The fastest bird is the peregrine <u>falcon</u>. It can fly at speeds of more than 217 miles per hour.
- The fastest runner is the <u>cheetah</u>. This hunting <u>leopard</u> can run at speeds of 60 miles per hour.
- The tallest animal is the giraffe. Some giraffes are 19 feet tall.
- The anaconda is the longest and heaviest snake. It can be 37 feet long and weigh more than 250 pounds.
- Hummingbirds are the smallest birds. An adult hummingbird can weigh less than a <u>penny</u>.
- The largest animal on land is the African elephant. It can weigh more than 6 tons.

C. Use a word from the Vocabulary Highlights to complete each of these sentences.

1. Those bricks _____ five pounds each.
2. I have a nickel, two dimes, a quarter, and a _____.
3. Troy is scared of any bug or _____.
4. The _____ is the largest animal in the sea.
5. Jean is as slow as an old _____.

(Go on to the next page.)

D. Decide whether each of these statements is true or false. If it is true, circle the T. If it is false, circle the F.

T F 1. A whale is larger than a shark.
T F 2. A cheetah is faster than a peregrine falcon.
T F 3. An ostrich is taller than a giraffe.
T F 4. Tortoises live longer than sharks.
T F 5. A walking stick is a kind of bird.
T F 6. Ostriches and falcons are birds.
T F 7. Zoologists are scientists who study animals.
T F 8. An anaconda is a long and heavy insect.
T F 9. The falcon is smaller than the hummingbird.
T F 10. Blue whales are larger than African elephants.

E. Decide which class each of the following animals belongs to. Use the following classes: fish, amphibians, birds, reptiles, insects, and mammals. Use a dictionary or an encyclopedia if you are not sure. The first one is done for you.

1. eagle _____bird_____
2. monkey _____
3. shark _____
4. lion _____
5. snake _____
6. flea _____
7. eel _____
8. dragonfly _____
9. sea horse _____
10. minnow _____
11. frog _____
12. crocodile _____
13. grasshopper _____
14. starling _____
15. whale _____
16. auk _____
17. toad _____
18. bat _____
19. kiwi _____
20. salamander _____

F. Find out about some other champions. Use an encyclopedia or other reference book if you need to. Use comparative and superlative forms of the adjective. The first one is done for you. Use it as a model for the others.

1. Long Rivers of the World
   Amazon _____longer_____
   Chang (Yangtze) _____long_____
   Nile _____longest_____

2. Big States in the United States
   California _____
   Alaska _____
   Texas _____

3. High Mountains of North America
   McKinley _____
   Orizaba (Citlaltepetl) _____
   Logan _____

4. Large Lakes of North America
   Michigan _____
   Superior _____
   Huron _____

Skill Sharpeners 3—Unit 12

Dear Dot

Dear Dot—

I am heartbroken. My boyfriend Rafael just broke up with me. He said that he has a new girlfriend. He says that she is prettier, funnier, nicer, and more intelligent than I am. He always told me that I was the prettiest, funniest, nicest, and most intelligent girl in the world. How could he change his mind like that? I still love him. He is the most attractive and interesting boy I have ever dated. What can I do to get him back?

Lorna

1. Why is Lorna heartbroken? _____

2. How does Rafael describe his new girlfriend? _____

3. What did he used to tell Lorna? _____

4. How does Lorna describe Rafael? _____

5. What does the word *attractive* mean in this letter? Circle your answer.

    a. bright   b. handsome   c. funny   d. frightening

6. What is your advice to Lorna? Discuss your answer in class. Then read Dot's answer and tell why you agree or disagree. Dot's advice is below.

Dear Lorna—

Nothing, and I don't know why you want him back, anyway. He has chosen another girl; it's time for you to see other boys. If Rafael thought you were the prettiest, funniest, and nicest girl in the world, I'm sure there are other boys who feel the same way about you—or would if they knew you. Forget about Rafael. Get out and meet some new boys—and probably nicer ones, too!

Dot

Write About It

Describe something that is the best—the best place you ever lived, the best movie you ever saw, the best meal you ever ate, etc.—in a paragraph or two. Describe everything about it. Use lots of superlative adjectives to describe why it was the best. And use lots of comparative adjectives to tell why it was better than other things of the same kind.

Verb Review: Past Tense (1)

Regular Verbs, present and past

a. End with *d* sound

agree/agreed	die/died	move/moved
allow/allowed	discover/discovered	order/ordered
amuse/amused	dry/dried	prepare/prepared
answer/answered	enjoy/enjoyed	remember/remembered
apply/applied	enter/entered	return/returned
arrive/arrived	fry/fried	save/saved
call/called	hurry/hurried	serve/served
carry/carried	learn/learned	stay/stayed
change/changed	listen/listened	study/studied
clean/cleaned	live/lived	travel/traveled
consider/considered	love/loved	try/tried
copy/copied	improve/improved	use/used
cry/cried	marry/married	worry/worried
describe/described		

b. End with *t* sound

accomplish/accomplished	finish/finished	talk/talked
ask/asked	increase/increased	type/typed
bake/baked	look/looked	walk/walked
brush/brushed	pack/packed	wash/washed
chase/chased	pick up/picked up	watch/watched
cook/cooked	practice/practiced	wax/waxed
dress/dressed	miss/missed	work/worked

c. End with sound of *id*

accept/accepted	decide/decided	paint/painted
attend/attended	demand/demanded	recommend/recommended
collect/collected	insist/insisted	start/started
complete/completed	invent/invented	suggest/suggested
correct/corrected	invite/invited	visit/visited
create/created	need/needed	want/wanted

NOTE: The past participles of regular verbs have the same form as the past tense. Example: *I study; I studied yesterday; I have studied all morning.*

On your paper write twenty sentences using as many of the verbs on this list in the past tense as you can. Try to use two or three verbs in each sentence. For example: *He was amused, but he agreed with me and allowed me to go.*

Skill Sharpeners 3—Verb Review

Verb Review: Past Tense (2)

Irregular Verbs, present, past, and past participle

am, is, are/was, were/been

begin/began/begun
bite/bit/bitten
bleed/bled/bled
blow/blew/blown
break/broke/broken
bring/brought/brought
build/built/built
buy/bought/bought

catch/caught/caught
choose/chose/chosen
come/came/come
cost/cost/cost
cut/cut/cut

do/did/did
drink/drank/drunk
drive/drove/driven

eat/ate/eaten

fall/fell/fallen
feed/fed/fed
feel/felt/felt
fight/fought/fought
find/found/found
fit/fitted (or fit)/fitted (or fit)
fly/flew/flown
freeze/froze/frozen

get/got/gotten
give/gave/given
go/went/gone
grow/grew/grown

have/had/had
hear/heard/heard
hide/hid/hid (or hidden)
hit/hit/hit
hold/held/held

keep/kept/kept
know/knew/known

lead/led/led
leave/left/left
lose/lost/lost

make/made/made
meet/met/met

pay/paid/paid
put/put/put

read/read/read
ride/rode/ridden
ring/rang/rung
rise/rose/risen
run/ran/run

say/said/said
see/saw/seen
sell/sold/sold
send/sent/sent
set/set/set
sew/sewed/sewn
shake/shook/shaken
shoot/shot/shot
show/showed/shown
sing/sang/sung
sit/sat/sat
sleep/slept/slept
speak/spoke/spoken
spend/spent/spent
split/split/split
stand/stood/stood
steal/stole/stolen
swim/swam/swum

take/took/taken
teach/taught/taught
tell/told/told
think/thought/thought

understand/understood/
  understood

wake/woke (or waked)/
  waked (or woken)
wear/wore/worn
win/won/won
write/wrote/written

On your paper write twenty sentences using as many of the verbs on this list in the past tense as you can. Try to use two or more verbs in each sentence. Then write twenty more sentences using the past participles of as many verbs as you can. Try to use different verbs from those you used in your past tense sentences.

Skill Objectives: Reviewing irregular verb forms, simple past tense and past participles, writing creative sentences

End of Book Test: Completing Familiar Structures

A. Circle the best answer.

Example: John is _____ than his sister.

    a. more old   (b. older)   c. more older   d. very older

1. Mary went to the library but her friends _____ go with her.

    a. weren't   b. aren't   c. don't   d. didn't

2. When did the plane arrive? It arrived _____.

    a. ten minutes ago   b. before ten minutes   c. in ten minutes   d. at ten minutes

3. Yesterday I _____ tired and stayed in bed.

    a. am   b. was   c. did   d. do

4. My friend _____ a new car.

    a. has   b. is having   c. have   d. is have

5. Cathy is _____ girl in the class.

    a. the most pretty   b. the prettiest   c. the more pretty   d. prettier than

6. I don't have much money but I have _____.

    a. little   b. a few   c. a little   d. few

7. Tom has been in the United States _____ 1978.

    a. for   b. until   c. after   d. since

8. How many times have you _____ the movie "Rocky"?

    a. see   b. saw   c. seeing   d. seen

9. I have _____ finished my homework.

    a. yet   b. been   c. already   d. until

10. Alexis is happy because he _____ a new car.

    a. has just bought   b. has bought yet   c. has boughten   d. has just buy

11. Bill _____ when I called him.

    a. was eating   b. ate   c. has eaten   d. is eating

12. Miami, Florida, is _____ than Boston.

    a. more warm   b. the warmest   c. warmer   d. more warmer

Skill Sharpeners 3—End of Book Test

End of Book Test: Completing Familiar Structures (continued)

13. The teacher told me _____ more often.

    a. to study   b. study   c. studying   d. studies

14. Robert cut _____ when he was shaving.

    a. him   b. his   c. himself   d. he

15. When Mr. Stevens was young, he _____ play football very well.

    a. could   b. can   c. was   d. did

16. Mary likes _____.

    a. traveler   b. traveling   c. to traveling   d. traveled

17. There are _____ cookies in the kitchen.

    a. a little   b. a big   c. a few   d. a many

18. When Martha was young, she _____ wash the dishes every night.

    a. can   b. had to   c. was   d. have to

19. When I arrived, there wasn't _____ in the office.

    a. somebody   b. anybody   c. nobody   d. body

20. The police _____ the robber.

    a. catching   b. to catch   c. caught   d. were caught

21. Mrs. Smith _____ at the bank since 1980.

    a. worked   b. working   c. works   d. has worked

22. Ellen can't talk on the telephone now because she _____ her hair.

    a. was washing   b. wash   c. is washing   d. washes

23. Janet can't drive a car because she _____ a license.

    a. hasn't had   b. doesn't have   c. don't have   d. didn't have

24. I bought these gloves _____.

    a. in two weeks   b. for two weeks   c. two weeks   d. two weeks ago

25. Dolores borrowed _____ books from the library.

    a. some   b. any   c. a little   d. much

Skill Sharpeners 3—End of Book Test

End of Book Test: Completing Familiar Structures (continued)

B. Read each sentence. Write the correct form of the verb on the line.

Examples: 1. Martha __went__ (go) to the bank yesterday.
2. Kenneth __goes__ (go) to the movies every day.

1. Tomorrow the hairdresser _____ (cut) my hair.

2. Last week George _____ (come) to class late.

3. My mother and father _____ (stay) at the Hilton Hotel now.

4. Linda _____ (work) at the bank many years ago.

5. John _____ (be) in the United States for ten years.

6. The President of the United States _____ (make) $200,000 a year.

7. When I arrived home, my mother _____ (make) lunch.

8. Harry and Larry _____ (see) the movie "Rocky" many times.

9. Paul _____ (sleep) at present.

10. My father _____ (get) up at six o'clock every morning.

Answer to puzzle on page 102.

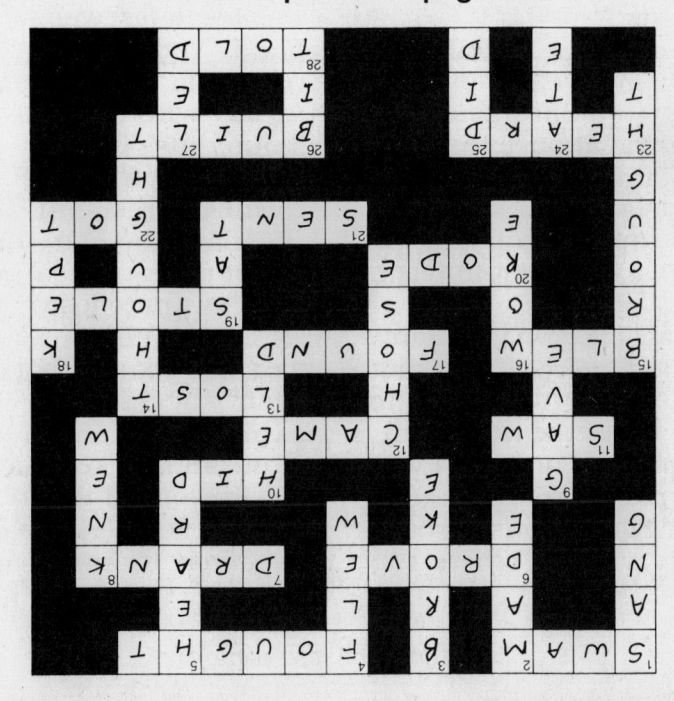

Skill Sharpeners 3—End of Book Test 125

End of Book Test: Reading Comprehension

Sacajawea

One of the most interesting and colorful women in the early history of the United States is Sacajawea, the Shoshone Indian princess. When Sacajawea was young, Indians from another tribe, the Minnetaree, kidnapped her from her home in the Rocky Mountains. They brought her to live in the central plains, near the Missouri River. Sacajawea was twelve or thirteen when the Minnetaree kidnapped her, old enough so that she never forgot her Shoshone heritage.

When Sacajawea was seventeen years old, a French trader, Pierre Charboneau, took her for his wife. The Indian girl left the Minnetaree and lived up river with her French husband. Together they worked along the Missouri River, trading with the different Indian tribes.

In 1804, something happened to change their lives. Captain Meriwether Lewis and Captain William Clark came to the village where Charboneau and Sacajawea lived. The two captains explained to the couple that they were heading west. They said that they were looking for a guide to take them through the unknown central lands and across the Rocky Mountains.

Sacajawea was very excited. She knew that these men were going to the home of her family, the Shoshone Indians. Sacajawea agreed at once to be the guide for the captains and their men. But it was too late in the year to begin a long journey. The captains told Sacajawea that the trip wasn't going to begin until spring.

In February, Sacajawea had a baby. Some of the soldiers were afraid that Sacajawea was not going to be able to make the trip. But when the time came, there were no problems. Sacajawea was ready and able to march with the men. She put the baby, Pompe, on her back and marched easily with the others.

Sacajawea led the men across the plains. She helped them to communicate with the Indians they met. She led them up and into the great Rocky Mountains. All the time, however, Sacajawea was looking for members of her tribe. After many weeks in the mountains, her dreams came true. Sacajawea and the explorers found the Shoshone village. To her surprise, her brother Cameahwait was the new chief of the tribe. Sacajawea was happy; she was finally with her family once again.

The captains were glad that Sacajawea was with her family, but they needed a guide to help them finish their job. They asked Sacajawea to continue with them on their journey. To their delight, she agreed. She and her husband and the baby accompanied Captains Lewis and Clark on the rest of the trip. They continued through the mountains and across the Northwest. The explorers didn't stop until they reached the Pacific Ocean.

Finally the work of exploring and map-making was over. The explorers were ready to return home. When they reached the Rocky Mountains, there was a sad farewell. Sacajawea, her husband, and Pompe the baby were not returning to the East. They were going to stay with the Shoshone in the Rocky Mountains. The two captains asked the family to reconsider. They wanted them to meet President Thomas Jefferson, the man who had sent the explorers on the journey. Sacajawea refused. She didn't want to lose her family again.

Lewis and Clark never forgot Sacajawea. They knew that they owed much of their success to her. When the two explorers returned to the East, they wrote and spoke of her often. Sacajawea became one of the most famous women of the 1800s. Her name and fame still live today in American history.

(Go on to the next page.)

A. **Answer the following questions. Use complete sentences.**

1. Who kidnapped Sacajawea? _____
   _____

2. Where did Lewis and Clark want to go? _____
   _____

3. Why did Sacajawea want to go with Lewis and Clark? _____
   _____

4. How did Sacajawea carry her baby on the long trip? _____
   _____

5. Why didn't Sacajawea return to the East with Lewis and Clark? _____
   _____

B. **Number these statements in the correct chronological order.**

   _____ Pierre Charboneau married Sacajawea.

   _____ Sacajawea found her family in the mountains.

   _____ Lewis and Clark came to the village of Sacajawea and Charboneau.

   _____ Sacajawea returned permanently to the Shoshone village.

   _____ The Minnetaree captured Sacajawea.

   _____ Sacajawea led the explorers through the Central Plains and into the Rocky Mountains.

   _____ The explorers saw the Pacific Ocean.

   _____ Sacajawea had a baby.

C. **Draw a conclusion to complete the sentence. Circle your answer.**

   Lewis and Clark traveled through the West because

   a. they were looking for gold.

   b. they were looking for Sacajawea's family.

   c. they were lost.

   d. they were making maps of the new territory.

D. **Write the letter of the quotation next to the speaker's name.**

   1. Sacajawea _____
   2. Charboneau _____
   3. Meriwether Lewis _____
   4. Cameahwait _____
   5. Thomas Jefferson _____

   a. "My sister, how I have missed you all these years. I never expected to see you again."

   b. "It is your job to explore this new territory and report back to me as soon as possible."

   c. "I must return to the shining mountains, the land of my people."

   d. "My partner and I need a guide to take us through the new land."

   e. "You are a beautiful woman, and I want you to be my wife."

Skill Sharpeners 3—End of Book Test

Skills Index

The pages listed below are those on which the skills are introduced and/or emphasized. Many of the skills appear, incidentally, on other pages as well.

Grammatical/Structural Skills

Adjectives
  adjective clauses, *who, where*, 61, 62
  comparatives, superlatives, 110–116, 118, 119, 120
  indefinite: *some, any*, 92
Adverbs
  already, yet, 42, 43, 44, 95
  ever, just, 52, 83, 99
  of frequency, 22, 27, 53
  of quantity, 24, 25, 29
Nouns
  non-count vs. count, 24, 25
  irregular plurals, 69, 98
Pronouns
  indefinite, 92
  subject, object, reflexive, 83, 103
Verbs
  future form: *going to*, 32, 37, 42, 43, 57
  future tense: *will*, 73, 115
  have/has/had to, 10, 27, 36, 51, 55
  liked/plan/want to, 10, 13, 18, 21, 57, 87
  modals: *can/can't, could/couldn't*, 15, 16, 50
  past tense, 10, 13, 15, 16, 18, 19, 21, 32, 36, 37, 42, 43, 46, 48, 53, 55, 58, 62, 64, 65, 68, 87, 93, 95, 96, 97, 99, 101, 102, 121, 122
  past progressive, 16, 21, 37, 40, 46, 62, 99, 122
  present tense, 9, 13, 15, 16, 22, 27, 32, 36, 37, 38, 46, 49, 80, 81, 99
  present perfect, 42, 43, 44, 46, 52, 53, 68, 86, 87, 93, 95, 99
  present perfect continuous, 84, 85, 86, 87, 99, 100, 108
  present progressive, 10, 11, 13, 16, 32, 37, 38, 40, 84, 122
  verb + gerund, 14, 16, 84, 86, 108

Reading Comprehension Skills

Cause and effect, 10, 27, 51, 55, 89, 93, 100
Classifying, 30, 60, 79, 90, 94, 98, 115, 119
Comparing and contrasting 14, 65, 115, 119, 120
Drawing conclusions, 27, 33, 41, 45, 47, 55, 59, 61, 63, 76, 77, 81, 89, 97, 102, 114, 115, 119
Drawing inferences, 31, 65, 71, 73, 76, 97, 107
Fact vs. opinion, 116
Following directions, 45, 78, 102
Identifying main idea and details, 11, 12, 19, 21, 38, 75, 104, 107, 115
Making generalizations, 10, 49, 60, 81
Making judgments, 21, 31, 41, 49, 57, 66, 74, 82, 91, 100, 109, 117, 120
Reading for details, 21, 26, 28, 29, 31, 39, 41, 46, 47, 49, 54, 55, 57, 58, 64, 65, 66, 68, 70, 71, 74, 78, 80, 81, 82, 86, 87, 88, 89, 91, 96, 97, 99, 100, 105, 108, 109, 117, 118, 119, 120
Sequencing, 12, 42, 43, 44, 53, 71, 97, 104, 107
Understanding words through context, 18, 19, 20, 21, 28, 29, 31, 38, 39, 41, 46, 47, 49, 54, 55, 57, 64, 65, 66, 67, 70, 71, 74, 80, 81, 82, 91, 96, 97, 100, 106, 107, 109, 118, 119, 120

Reading in the Content Areas

Math
  charts, tables, graphs, 23, 59, 60, 99, 114
  fractions, percentages, prices, weights, 23, 26, 60
  word problems, 23, 26, 60, 86, 99, 114
Science
  animal classification, 119
  chemistry, 88, 89
  health, 28, 29, 38, 39, 76, 77, 78
  inventions, 54, 55, 65
  space study, 68, 70, 71
  water cycle, weather, 80, 81, 104
Social Studies
  career education, 34, 35, 115
  graphs and maps, 45, 59, 114, 117
  U.S. economics, 114, 117
  U.S. history, 12
    Declaration of Independence, 46
    exploration and settlement, 96, 97, 106, 107
    famous Americans 18, 54, 55, 68
    immigration, 59, 60
    railroads, 64, 65

Study Skills

Choosing correct definitions, 17, 18, 28, 38, 46, 54, 64, 70, 80, 88, 96, 106, 118
Getting information from graphics
  bar, line, pie graphs, 59, 114
  charts and tables, 22, 23, 52, 53, 60, 99, 104, 114
  labels, prescriptions, 78
  maps, 45, 81, 117
  menus, schedules, 26, 105
  timelines, 12, 42
Identifying library resources, 72, 94
  doing research, 60, 71, 76, 81, 89, 94, 97, 119
Outlining, 19, 47
Plotting information
  bar, line, pie graphs, 60, 114
  charts, 10, 29, 52, 65, 104, 111
Taking notes, 52, 89

Survival Skills

Discussing "Help Wanted" ads, 115
Filling out applications, 34, 35
Learning about health/illness, 76
  medical prescriptions, products, and labels, 77, 78
  vitamins, calorie charts, 23, 28, 29
Learning about weather maps and forecasts, 80, 81
Reading a menu, 26
Reading a subway map, 45
Reading a TV schedule, 105
Writing friendly letters, 75, 100

Vocabulary Development

Community places, 10, 33, 41, 54, 58, 61, 62, 77, 79, 87, 98, 108, 115
Cities, states, countries, 10, 12, 13, 15, 18, 37, 46, 53, 54, 59, 60, 79, 80, 81, 87, 90, 94, 96, 97, 99, 106, 107, 108, 112, 113, 116, 117
Feelings, 21, 31, 41, 49, 57, 58, 66, 74, 75, 82, 91, 93, 94, 100, 109, 120
Health, 28, 29, 33, 38, 76, 77, 78, 79, 89, 116
Language on special forms, 34, 35, 46, 78, 115
Numbers (dates, fractions, measurements, percents), 12, 23, 33, 38, 59, 60, 70, 86, 99, 106, 114
Occupations, 16, 33, 34, 54, 61, 64, 67, 76, 79, 80, 86, 87, 88, 98, 106, 108, 115, 117, 118
Recognizing antonyms, synonyms, homophones, 20, 30, 56, 98
Tools and machines, 11, 54, 64, 65, 68, 79
Understanding prefixes, 63
Weather, 15, 79, 80, 81, 89, 104, 114, 116

Writing Skills

Answering questions about self, 15, 34, 35, 50, 73
Autobiographical paragraphs, 31, 58, 66, 91, 104
  explaining opinions, personal decisions, 57, 59, 65, 82, 104, 117
Combining sentences, 27, 62, 84
Describing data from charts, graphs, 22, 52, 81
Descriptive paragraphs, 11, 49, 66, 113, 120
Fictional paragraphs, 74, 75, 100
Filling out applications, 34, 35
Questions, 13, 15, 24, 25, 87, 108
Using words in creative sentences, 40, 48, 73, 101, 110, 121, 122
Writing definitions, 61, 81
Writing directions, 41, 45, 109
Writing friendly letters, 75, 100
Writing short research reports, 71, 76, 81, 89, 97